H
abou

M000300804

TALES OF THE SACRED HEART (Novel)

". . . like Joyce's *Dubliners,* only more interrelated."
—Susan McGury, DePaul University

"An urban fantasy that makes the struggle between good and evil a lot of fun to watch. A great read—I hated to see it end."
—Shirley Hardy-Leonard, 1995 Disney Fellow, author of *Miss Dessa*

"Bravo! A wonderfully idiosyncratic and lyrical tale. Weaves together the heartfelt and the humorous with straight-from-the-street characters who place you under their spell."
—Colleen Delegan, writer for NBC and ABC, screenwriter for *Born Guilty* and *The Last Witch of England*

CALLING OZ (Screenplay)

"Very clever and very funny. The characters and set-up are pure gold."
—Danny Rubin, author of *Groundhog Day*

"Amazing . . . the cleverest premise I've seen in a long while . . . sharp literacy and command of language that is extraordinary."
—Richard Walter, Screenwriting Chairman, UCLA, author of *The Whole Picture*

"A truly delightful comedy . . . wonderfully witty."
—Charlotte Gusay, The Charlotte Gusay Literary Agency (Los Angeles)

"Superb writing."
—Robert Cope, President, The Writers Foundation (Orlando, FL)

"A very funny story."
—Stuart Gordon's Red Hen Productions

Here's what people are saying
about Melanie Villines' writing . . .

CALLING OZ (Screenplay)

"Original."
—Dana Scanlan, Kushner-Locke Productions

"Wonderful."
—Melanie Ray, Mustang Pictures

"Extraordinary writing."
—Michael Farrand, Empire Productions

CRIME OF INNOCENCE (Teleplay, Cowriter)

"A rich, thought-provoking script."
—Daniel Ruth, *Chicago Sun-Times*

"Deals with an important and sensitive subject . . .
superbly written."
—Gordon Walek, *Daily-Herald (Illinois)*

"Compelling."
—Clifford Terry, *Chicago Tribune*

PRIVATE MEETINGS IN PUBLIC PLACES (Stage Play)

"Fresh and funny."
—Richard Christiansen, *Chicago Tribune*

"Glows with creativity."
—Tom Valeo, *Daily-Herald (Illinois)*

"Genuine honesty and wit."
—*Chicago Reader*

TALES OF THE SACRED HEART

a novel

Melanie Villines

11/10/03
Heather — Hope you
enjoy this Chicago tale.
Best regards,
Melanie Villines

BOGFIRE®
Celebrating the Creative Spirit™

Libertyville, Illinois

© January 1999 by Melanie Villines
First edition

Library of Congress Cataloging-in-Publication Data
Villines, Melanie
    Tales of the sacred heart: a novel / Melanie Villines. — 1st ed.
    p. cm.
    ISBN 0-9668405-0-X
    1. Tales of the Sacred Heart
    PS3572.I389 T35 1999
    813' .54—dc21   98-32195
                                        CIP

Cover art: *The Astrologer,* anonymous watercolored wood engraving, circa 1768-1784. © 1998 PhotoDisc, Inc.

Cover design by Connie Scanlon, BogFire Inc.
Typeset in Garamond

Published by BogFire Inc.
1840 Industrial Drive, Suite 240
Libertyville, IL 60048-9400
847-918-9698
fax: 847-918-0725
email: bogfire@interaccess.com
www.bogfire.com

For my grandmother
Dwilla Lewis DuBouchet
(1887-1977)

and my aunt
Esther DuBouchet Schneiter
(1915-1997)

two great storytellers

God is really another artist. He invented the giraffe,
the elephant, and the cat. He has no real style. He just
goes on trying other things.

Pablo Picasso

Table of Contents

PART ONE:

THE VOICE OF HEAVEN

CHAPTER 1

The Heart of God

The yellow poster screamed "MIRACLES! MIRACLES! MIRACLES!" at Norma Villalobos as she huddled on the windy elevated platform. Norma noticed more and more signs like this in her Isabel Park neighborhood every day. Sacred Heart church was closing, and the revivalists had already picked up the scent.

When the Cardinal handed down his decision, Norma was already questioning her faith. No longer did she slam her door in the faces of Jehovah's Witnesses. No longer did she think the Mormons were conquistadors in disguise. No longer did she laugh at the TV preachers.

Norma missed the drama of the old church ways. She missed the Latin Mass. She missed the rituals. She missed the daily doses of incense. She hated the guitar mass. She hated the sign of peace. She hated seeing the priest working with his face to the crowd.

Santa Maria, they were even threatening to replace the candles with electric wicks!

Norma Villalobos was ripe for the revival meeting that was setting up camp in her Chicago neighborhood's VFW hall.

* * * * *

The Cardinal wanted to put Father Jeremiah Flynn out to pasture. The Pastor was not a good soldier. He questioned the official word.

Sacred Heart was falling apart. Worse, it was dangerous. Plaster fell from the ceiling like hail. The Wisniewski woman and the entire

Lopez family had received direct shots to the head. During a Baptism, the crumbling plaster had rained right into an infant's mouth! The church's beams were rotting. The foundation was sinking. The roof was full of holes.

The building inspectors said the church had to be repaired or shut down. The Cardinal could find much better uses for a million dollars. Sacred Heart would close.

But Pastor Flynn would not accept the decision.

"Sacred Heart is a landmark. The first replica of St. Peter's Basilica erected in the United States," Father Flynn shouted in the cozy quiet of the Cardinal's study.

"It has outlived its usefulness," the Cardinal replied.

"But the Masses are filled to capacity every Sunday."

"The collection plate does not reflect high attendance."

"The people are poor, Your Eminence."

"Yes, the neighborhood is not what it once was."

"The neighborhood is what it has always been—a home for immigrants."

"My parents were immigrants," said the Cardinal, "yet they not only managed to give to the church—they built the church. As you know, it was my father's idea to create a replica of St. Peter's."

"And, with your family legacy, you would still shut the doors?"

"Sentiment plays no part in these things, Father Flynn. This is business."

"Give us a chance to raise the money."

"Even if Sacred Heart were repaired, there isn't enough coming in every week to even pay the light bill."

"What would it take to make you change your mind?" asked Father Flynn. "A miracle?"

* * * * *

As she waited for the A-train, Norma bent down and read the small print on the yellow poster taped to the newspaper vending machine.

Church of Fire presents Sister Merlina Talbott, Saturday, Jan. 9th, at 7:30 p.m. Come one, come all to an evening with God. Sister Talbott will help you find Jesus. Sing and Dance in the Spirit, Speak in Tongues. The Lord will touch you, and you will feel His Holy Presence by being Slain in the Spirit. Feel the Power of the Almighty as Sister Talbott brings your prayer requests to the Throne of the Most High. She will Lay Hands on the sick, on the poor, on the depressed. Come in a sinner, leave a Saint. Don't miss this once-in-a-lifetime chance to share God's Presence with One of His Most Anointed!!!

Though Norma was only forty-five and in good health, her back was stiff and her eyes ached as she stood up after reading the wordy poster. Yes, she thought, you get a backache and an eye twitch from reading the poster, and you have to go to the faith healer to have her take the pain away.

Despite her cynical thoughts, Norma was intrigued. What harm could it do? At the very least, she would have an interesting story to tell at Julio's twenty-fifth birthday party the following day.

* * * * *

On Saturday, January 9th, Julio was just getting in gear for his long evening out. When he stepped into the bathroom to take a shower, he was surprised to see his mother putting on lipstick. She was dressed up and was wearing a hat.

"Where are you going?" he asked.

"Out," Norma said.

"Where?"

"To see a friend."

"Who?"

"Maria."

"Maria?"

"Please, Julio, I'll be late."

She picked up her purse, and headed for the door.

"Wait," he said. "I'll walk you. It's not safe out there."

"It's not safe because of you and the Latin Lords," Norma said, bringing up a sore subject.

"We protect the neighborhood," Julio said quietly. "That's all."

"I have to leave," she said, and did.

* * * * *

Julio had been the leader of the Latin Lords for two years, and now he wanted out. But quitting wasn't so easy. He didn't want his mother to think that her harping had done any good. The next thing he knew, she'd be throwing out his leather jacket and making him wear one of those insulated vests that make you look like a turtle. The story would have to be good.

He was afraid to leave for other more obvious reasons. You didn't just quit the Latin Lords. Membership was a lifetime appointment.

After all these years, Julio had learned one hard-to-admit lesson: He was his mother's son. He needed a purpose in life. He wanted to marry a nice girl, buy a nice brick bungalow on the northwest side, and have a couple of nice kids. He wanted to have a finished basement, where he could watch Bears' games and drink beer with his working buddies. He wanted a real job, a real family, and a real life.

But it would take a miracle to get him out of the gang.

* * * * *

At the VFW hall, Norma took her place among the motley crowd that had assembled on the old brown padded folding chairs. She thought it odd that the VFW people had not removed the set of drums that sat prominently in the front of the room. Probably left over from last night's wedding party, she thought. Next to the drums sat a wicker laundry basket. The floors were unswept, there were cobwebs in every corner. This lack of order disturbed Norma. She wondered how God could consent to visit this messy place.

From her seat in the last row, Norma scanned the gathering. She hoped there wasn't anyone who would recognize her, but she quickly realized that was too much to ask. In the very front row sat her next-door neighbors, the Sikes family. Sitting between Tyler and Deeanna Sikes was their ten-year-old, Charlie, exhibiting the full range of tics, involuntary movements, and strange noises that had led the family to a series of doctors, who had given them no hope for the boy's misery. Now they were here in the front row hoping for a miracle.

* * * * *

As the runty seventh child of a couple of poor Indiana farmers, Tyler Sikes had been picked on mercilessly by his brothers, sisters, schoolmates, and neighbors. Even the animals seemed to have it in for him. He was forever being kicked, stepped on, bitten, peed on, and chased by the farm's horses, cows, dogs, and cats. When Tyler had to collect eggs, the hens were at the ready, beaks poised like sabers—daring him to reach into their nests.

Tyler slowly withdrew into a world where he was a titan, the most powerful, handsome man in the universe. He did great deeds, slew giants, and all the beautiful women in the world were his for the taking. He just knew that if he were big and handsome nothing bad would happen to him. These fantasies were the train Tyler rode throughout his childhood. Somehow they were powerful enough to take him to the end of the line. It was a miracle he had reached adulthood still in one piece.

It was also a miracle that Deeanna had agreed to bring Charlie here tonight. Tyler and Deeanna hadn't been getting along. Despite her devout Catholicism, Deeanna had been talking the "D" word. Tyler knew that nothing less than a miracle would make Deeanna change her mind.

* * * * *

"Hallelujah, Brothers and Sisters," said a booming voice from the back of the hall. Norma turned and watched as Sister Talbott made her way down the center aisle.

The woman had to be six feet tall, not counting her foot-high beehive hairdo and spike-heeled shoes. She wore a white choir robe that billowed out behind her as she vaulted down the aisle. Sister Talbott was followed by a short man in a tuxedo, who took a seat behind the drums.

When she arrived at the front of the room, Sister Talbott raised her arms and said: "Welcome, Brothers and Sisters. I speak for Brother Talbott and myself when I say we are filled with the Joy of the Lord this evening!"

"Amen," said many voices in the crowd.

"Hold hands, Brothers and Sisters, and let us pray," Sister Talbott said as she folded her hands palm to palm.

Norma pretended she didn't hear the part about holding hands. The sign of peace in the new Catholic ways was bad enough. But holding hands throughout an entire prayer? Norma closed her eyes and folded her hands. But two zealots pried her hands apart and held them tightly while Sister Talbott spoke the invocation.

By the time Sister Talbott got to "Amen," Norma was overwhelmed with relief and yanked her hands away from her fellow worshipers as if she were removing babies from kidnappers. Norma had a deep-seeded fear of strangers' germs.

"And now, my Friends, let us sing 'What a Friend We Have in Jesus.'" Sister Talbott turned and nodded to her husband, who immediately began to bang on the drums.

The preacher's voice was loud and strong as she led the singers through the old hymn. The crowd had trouble figuring out how to sing along with the drums, but Sister Talbott used her giant's voice to pull them through the crashing beats.

Never in her life had Norma heard of singing spiritual songs to drums and drums alone. Once she'd heard an African Mass called "Missa Luba" on Henry Purcell's program on WHVN-FM. But that was Africa. This was America, this was Norma's neighborhood, Isabel Park—bordered by Sacred Heart church on one end and the high red and white tower of WHVN-FM, the voice of heaven, on the other.

This was Isabel Park, only twenty minutes by subway from downtown Chicago, but worlds away from the higher life. This was where immigrants set down their first roots—where Poles, Eastern Europeans, and Latinos lived side by side, brought together by their poverty, lack of English, and their belief in the Catholic faith.

As Brother Talbott continued to beat on the drums, Norma wondered why. The songs could easily be sung with no musical accompaniment. But perhaps this was part of the message: boom, boom, boom on the drums—like God's heart beating right here in the room.

* * * * *

Henry Purcell came to work one day and found photos of the ad manager's children on his desk. He looked around. All of his things were gone. In their place were golf trophies and Arbitron rating books. He finally located his belongings in the boiler room.

Next, they changed his drivetime show (5-6 p.m. M-F) to the graveyard (11 p.m.-12M SA-SU). Just like that, Henry had lost his home and he had lost his flock. And despite his gift for words, Henry was unable to get through to the station management.

Henry's show, during its regular time period, had been getting decent ratings. The show wasn't gaining, but it wasn't losing, either. The shares were stable and predictable. The advertisers were long-standing and loyal. Why, then, would they give him the ax?

During his seventy-odd years, Henry had acquitted himself as much more than a talk show host on WHVN-FM, "the voice of heaven." His interests, knowledge, and experience were wide and varied. He had written several mainstream sociological works, and had won the Pulitzer prize not once, but twice. Henry wasn't just a big fish in a small pond—he was a big fish, period.

Henry *was* the voice of heaven.

* * * * *

". . . take it to the Lord in prayer." The song ended with Brother Talbott crashing the cymbal.

Norma hoped that would be the end to the singing. She didn't like the drums and she didn't know the words to Protestant songs. This was even worse than the guitar Mass.

"Brothers and Sisters," began Sister Talbott, "maybe you're wondering why I'm here in these humble surroundings, instead of greeting you from the magnificent hall of a stately hotel or from a traditional revival tent set on lush, verdant fairgrounds that speak to the Glory of God's Creation. Wonder no more, Brothers and Sisters. It's because of the DEVIL!"

The crowd started to murmur. When Sister Talbott had milked the moment to its fullest, she went on.

"Yes, the DEVIL, Praise the Lord. The Church of Fire had been traveling the country, holding meetings in a state-of-the-art revival tent made from the latest high-tech synthetic material. The tent kept out heat, it kept out cold. Wherever we went, our meetings were like a little bit of Eden set down to comfort God's Children. We were holding meetings and taking collections for a missionary effort to Darkest Africa. And then, it happened. One night near Topeka, Kansas, as we were walking across a field of wheat, we saw our beloved tent, the tent we had scrimped and saved for—and there it was in Flames!"

"Ohhhh," gasped the crowd.

"Yes, my Friends, our tent was being devoured by the DEVIL'S HELLISH FIRE! Praise the Lord, there were no people inside. But all our savings, the money we'd collected to travel to Darkest Africa was in a trunk under the stage. Nothing was saved, everything was burned, burned, burned—right to the ground."

The crowd broke out in a sweat. As poor people who lived in rundown buildings with bad wiring, they were always worrying about fires. If God could let this happen to Sister Talbott, what about those who were much, much lower on the anointed scale?

This was Norma's first non-Catholic service. She thought the proceedings would follow the same basic format as they did at Sacred Heart—except they wouldn't pray to the Virgin Mary. So far, they had said a prayer and had sung a song. Were they already at the sermon? If so, they were not talking about messages from the Bible. They were talking about Sister Talbott's bad luck. Norma felt that Sister Talbott was not living up to her advance advertising. Where was the Dancing in the Spirit? Where was the Speaking in Tongues?

Where were the Miracles?

* * * * *

The Cardinal hadn't counted on resistance. But there they were every night on the news, every morning in the paper. The "Save Sacred Heart" contingent.

The Cardinal did not need bad publicity. He was up for a special appointment in Rome, and if word got out that he couldn't

13

handle things at home, how was he going to convince his colleagues that he could handle Vatican business?

Yet, he couldn't lose face and change his decision. He would have to think of a way out.

At the press conference, the Cardinal's aide read a one-sentence statement. "If Sacred Heart parish can raise one million dollars for the repairs by the end of the year, the church can remain open."

The Cardinal believed there was no way in hell this would happen.

* * * * *

". . . and so, Brothers and Sisters, God has led me to ask for your help in rebuilding His Temple. He has sent his Dear Angel Uriel to help me tonight. Uriel will shine colored lights over the heads of those whom God has chosen to contribute to our missionary work."

All eyes turned to the back of the room, expecting that the Angel was about to make a grand entrance.

"No, my Friends, the Angel is right here, standing beside me. Only I can see Him, for God has opened mine eyes, His Wonders to receive."

Sister Talbott walked up the center aisle and began to point at various people. Perhaps drawing her inspiration from the K-Marts where many in the audience shopped, Sister Talbott said: "The angel is shining a blue light over your head. This means you have twenty dollars for God. Take it to the front of the room and lay it in the wicker basket."

As the blue light crowd made its way to the basket, the Angel was already shining orange lights over those with ten dollars for God. This was followed by many, many people who were flooded in purple light (five dollars). Others dug dollar bills out of their pockets and purses under a green angelic spotlight. Sister Talbott saw silver sparks over the heads of the remaining people, and advised them to deposit all their spare change into the basket.

As he removed the five-dollar bill from his wallet, Tyler thought he, too, could see a purple light. Sure'd be nice and handy to have an angel guide, he figured. I could quit the mini-mart. And then, making a leap from his days of dreaming he was a titan, he thought: What would it be like to *be* an angel?

The collection took a lot of time. Blue and orange and purple and green lights, plus silver sparks, people walking back and forth in the aisles—even Norma coughed up a dollar. She didn't believe any of it for a minute, but was smart enough to know that there was just a fraction of a chance that it was true. A dollar was a small price to pay for peace of mind.

A smiling Brother Talbott picked up the jingling laundry basket and made his way out of the hall. A few moments later, from her place at the back of the room, Norma heard a car trunk close with a satisfied thud. Brother Talbott returned as his wife was beginning to lay hands on the sick.

Norma watched as Sister Talbott said what sounded like "Urey Anna Banda" as she slapped one hand against the supplicant's forehead and another on the back of the person's head. "In the Name of Jesus," Sister Talbott crooned, eyes closed. She removed her hands, then went on to the next waiting soul.

Norma watched as, one by one, the people got their heads banged and then staggered back to their seats. Sometimes, people were so filled with the Holy Spirit that they dropped like felled logs to the floor, where they shook and cried and muttered strange words. New people had to step over these bodies as they brought their troubles to Sister Talbott's Anointed Hands. While Sister Talbott worked, Brother Talbott placed tiny blankets over the knees of the women in skirts who had been Slain in the Spirit.

Norma noticed that so far the infirmities had been of the invisible variety: cancer, heart trouble, depression, gallstones. Who knew if they had been healed or not? It was just like when you went to the brujo and he swept your body with herbs. Who could tell if it worked?

But when Norma saw who had the next appointment with Sister Talbott's Anointed Hands, she smiled. The boy, with his strange movements and embarrassing obscenities, was someone she knew.

* * * * *

For all his powers, the brujo was having little success with one particular case. Manuel had brushed the area around the child's

body with basil and sage, had instructed Emilia's r
candle dedicated to St. Angela at the foot of the
she slept, had prescribed herbs to be added to her soup, had
the child's hands and feet with alum stones, and had later melted the
stones and buried the liquid. He had made the child sit with closed
eyes while he swirled frankincense around her. He had rung bells
over her body. He had recited prayers in Latin, and instructed her
mother to pay the priest for thirty days of Masses.
He had doused the child with precious drops of holy water from a
church in Mexico City. Still, it had done no good. The child still
scooped up handsful of dirt and gulped them down.

Manuel Morales was beginning to doubt his powers. If only he
could get the child to eat something besides dirt, perhaps there
would be hope. Her fixation would be broken. If only he could get
her to swallow goldfish, or nibble on pigeon feathers, or eat sand, or
taste ashes, maybe, just maybe, he could hope for a miraculous cure.

* * * * *

When Sister Talbott got her first look at Charlie, Norma
detected a momentary fluster. Here, at last, was a visible infirmity,
and the whole crowd would be scrutinizing the results.

Charlie held back, but his parents nudged him closer to
the Sister.

"Blessed be the little children," said Sister Talbott, as she scoped out the full range of Charlie's tics and gyrations.

"Bitch!" said Charlie.

Deeanna Sikes started to cry. Tyler Sikes held his wife's elbow and made an effort to keep a stony front.

Sister Talbott's hands sprang up and banged both sides of the boy's head. "In the Name of Jesus," she said as she squeezed Charlie's head harder and harder. She released her hands and looked at the boy, who continued to thrash and jerk. Once again, she grasped the boy's head, she called on Jesus, she squeezed, then stepped away to view her handiwork. Nothing. Undaunted, Sister Talbott tried again. And again and again. The boy's forehead was a mass of red splotches that were already beginning to turn blue.

Suddenly, Sister Talbott stepped back, closed her eyes, and raised her face skyward. "I am receiving a message from God. The Lord is talking to me. Telling me about this boy. I am seeing inside his entire body. The Lord is revealing to me that this boy HAS LEUKEMIA!"

Deeanna Sikes sobbed. Even the stoic Tyler Sikes had silent tears streaming down his face.

"In the Name of Jesus," Sister Talbott said, and quickly removed her hands. She looked at the boy. "Son, you have just been cured of leukemia. Praise Jesus!"

Tyler and Deeanna led their jerking child back to his seat. They were grateful that the inspired woman had detected the insidious problem and had cured their poor child. They could live with the tics.

The audience to this drama was spellbound. The boy had been cured of LEUKEMIA! And he didn't even know he had it! Praise the Lord!

It was a miracle.

* * * * *

That night, Norma had a series of vivid dreams about Sister Merlina Talbott. In one, Sister Talbott was a living, moving Statue of Liberty off the shore of Lake Michigan. In another, Sister Talbott was the Virgin Mary appearing to three farmer's children in a field of wheat near Topeka, Kansas. Then Sister Talbott was Wonder Woman from TV. Again, Merlina Talbott was Betsy Ross, sewing the American flag as the Angel Uriel held the material.

All of the dreams were accompanied by a musical score: drums beating and throbbing in the background, like the heart of God.

CHAPTER 2

Quantum Popular Mechanics

"Is the Pope Polish?" Tyler replied, when the customer asked if the price of cigarettes would keep going up.

As Leszek Paprocki waited in line to pay for his milk, all the indignities he'd suffered as an immigrant seemed to amass around this insult to the Patriarch from his native land. He could not let it pass. He had to do something.

"How you doin' tonight, Lester?" said Tyler, full of good humor and unaware that he had just placed the last straw on Leszek's fragile psyche.

Leszek, or Lester, as his blue repairman's shirt identified him, considered his options. He could insult Tyler's nationality, but a couple of hundred years of intermarriage between the Irish and Germans and English and God-knew-what else had distilled any recognizable trace of bloodlines from Tyler's blue-white skin and flat-boned face.

Next, Leszek considered insulting Tyler's religion, but he'd seen the hillbilly at Sacred Heart every Sunday with his blue-skinned, white-haired daughter and his unfortunate, spastic son. There, faithfully, every single Sunday. Leszek couldn't even accuse Tyler of being a hypocrite.

When Lester failed to respond and made no move to pay for his milk, Tyler figured the man was trying to decide between the *Enquirer* and *Star*, and motioned to those in line behind Les to move up.

As the possibilities raced through Leszek's mind, the milk sweated in his hand and dripped a pool of water on the floor.

The other customers left, took their Twinkies, Diet Coke, and Wonder Bread, and went home. Tyler resumed the book that he'd pulled from the rack on the ice cream cooler. It was then that Leszek hit on an idea.

"You have no taste in reading materials," he stated, and felt a warm glow of satisfaction flow through his chest.

"Say what?" Tyler asked, as he placed his index finger on his spot and looked up.

"You are reading trash," said Leszek boldly, as he hefted the milk onto the counter.

"I read what I want to read," Tyler said, still cheerful, glad, in fact, for the chitchat.

"Your mind will turn to garbage," responded Leszek, carefully removing bills from his wallet.

"What are you gettin' at, Les?"

"I am saying, I am telling you that you are feeding your mind with empty words, with stupid, mindless stories."

And then, pointing at the air to indicate the rock music blaring over the loudspeakers, Leszek said, "You listen to music that sounds like a thousand piss cans rattling against each other in a broken-down washing machine."

"Now, Les, it's a free country. That's why people like you come here. Cause we can read anything or listen to anything we damn well please."

"That is why this country is all a mess. There is no education, no culture. Just junk food for the body and the soul."

Tyler put down his book and sighed. You can never get any peace, he thought. It's always something. If you're not being held up, your boss is yelling at you, or your wife is in a bad mood, or you go home and find mouse droppings in your corn flakes. And now this guy. Why did he have to do it? I gave him every chance to shut his trap and get the hell out of here. But, no. He's gotta keep at it, till he gives me no choice.

"Buddy, nobody was losing sleep over your not being here. If you don't like it, why don't you just go back where you came from?"

But Leszek had heard this before, and he was prepared.

"Why don't *you* go back where you came from—go back to a cave!" Leszek smiled. The warm glow from his chest had spread to his back and neck. He felt as if he'd just returned from a ten-day fishing trip.

Tyler closed his book and stepped out from behind the counter. He walked up to Leszek and stared straight in his eyes.

"What's the matter, Buddy? That pretty wife of yours cut you off?"

Pretty wife! The nerve of this inbred hillbilly, thought Leszek. Scenes passed through his head. Danuta entering the mini-mart to buy bread, wearing the blue cotton dress that showed off her figure, and this . . . this . . . lowlife trash reader looking up from a lewd passage in some smutty novel and thinking bad thoughts about her. Danuta bending over to tie Sandra's shoe, and this no-class mini-mart clerk looking down her blouse! Pretty wife! And what was this?

Something about sexual healing coming over the speakers—the low, suggestive voice of the singer sounding like he was about to . . . .

* * * * *

Danuta replaced the wire coat hangers with the plastic kind that cost ten cents each. The wire hangers had picked up WHVN's signal perfectly, but now there was only a faint mumble from the hinges of the closets.

She had replaced the silverware with plastic; this made her feel like a peasant. Wherever she could, Danuta substituted a non-conducting material for metal. But there was still the toaster and other necessary metal objects in the house.

Father Flynn had blessed the house, but it had done no good. Danuta's days were still spent alone in a house filled with unwanted sounds.

She couldn't drive, she couldn't work, her child was in school, Leszek was always at one of his many jobs, and she couldn't speak the native language. Danuta walked through the house, a ghost among ghosts.

This is not what Danuta had expected when, after three long years, Leszek had sent for her and the child. "I have bought a house in Amerika!" he had written. A house, it turned out, that was right across the alley from WHVN-FM, the voice of heaven.

* * * * *

Only seconds had passed, but the scenes brewing in Leszek's skull could have filled the entire rack of cheap novels that blazed out at him from their circular stand atop the ice cream cooler.

For his part, Tyler wanted to forget the whole thing and get back to the Nigel Clive book, which he'd thought was one of his beloved spy novels, but turned out to be a nonfiction work that explained the concepts of physics in everyday terms. The book also showed how mastery could be attained over daily events. When Leszek had launched his attack, Tyler had been in the middle of the chapter about visualizing what you want in life. Maybe he could try it out right now.

* * * * *

When the doorbell rang, Danuta was tempted to hide in the bathroom. She hated when somebody came to the door while Leszek was away. It was always a meter reader or a precinct captain or a telephone repairman, and they always talked fast and, when she didn't respond, looked at her as if she had boiled potatoes for brains.

Danuta peeked through the curtains and saw an old man. He didn't see her looking at him. She studied his eyes, the sad eyes of a soldier returning from war. She opened the door.

"I'm eliciting contributions for the repair work that will return Sacred Heart church to its former glory. And I'm collecting signatures to help Henry Purcell, a victim of our society's woeful ageism. Could you please help?" said Jarvis.

Danuta understood "please" and "help." She thought the man perhaps had suffered a flat tire and needed to phone a garage. She opened the door and indicated the phone on the end table. Jarvis gave Danuta a puzzled look, but entered.

It had been a year since Judge Jarvis's release from jail and his heart surgery. He had found a new purpose in life working to save Sacred Heart and Henry Purcell. He had joined a poetry club and had even won a prize for best sonnet. His days were filled, he looked good, he was healthy—altogether, he was a lot better off than he'd been a year ago, when he was sitting on the bench, taking bribes, and about to be cited in the government's Operation Bloodhound probe.

* * * * *

Leszek's rage made him aware of veins he had never noticed in his body. Blood gushed, throbbed, and beat through a million large and small passages along the surface of his skin and deep within him. Slowly, his hands formed into fists at his sides.

Tyler watched as Leszek raised his hands. Shit, he thought. I do not want to fight this Polack. They eat three squares a day, 365 days a year. They're strong. They're healthy. He'll beat the bejeezus out of me.

Leszek's hands seemed to rise in slow motion. Tyler had once taken a TV correspondence course, and had learned that there are twenty-four separate frames in one second of film. Tyler watched Leszek's fists as they moved closer, and saw twenty-four separate tiny movements in each second that the man's hands rose. Tyler watched, fascinated. It was as if he were able to see into the guts of the world's clock—time oozing out, right before his very eyes.

Tyler snapped out of it and moved his eyes away from Leszek's hands. Even though time had slowed down, eventually Les would hit his mark, and Tyler's brains would be all over the rack of Ding Dongs and HoHos.

Quickly, Tyler tried to remember what Nigel Clive had recommended in a case like this. Use physics to master the material world, Nigel had written. But how? Tyler thought of picking up the book and thumbing through it, but didn't know if time would speed up again and he'd find himself in an unscheduled appointment with Leszek's big, meaty, Polack hands.

* * * * *

Jarvis immediately noticed the music that exuded from every crack and crevice of Danuta's house. He also noticed the Polish newspaper, the same one he bought for his landlady every morning, and the gilt-framed photos of foreign-looking people. His years as a judge had given Jarvis the ability to quickly size up situations. This lady doesn't speak much English, he thought.

"Where is the music?" he asked.

Danuta made a sweeping motion with her hands.

"Everywhere," she said.

"Do you have a special kind of radio?" Jarvis asked.

Danuta walked toward the kitchen and pointed out the back window. Jarvis stood beside her and looked out. The window framed a portion of WHVN's red and white tower.

"That is the station," he said.

"Yes," Danuta replied, "the radio. It come in here, my house. Music everywhere."

A house where music always plays, thought Jarvis. And one station—the voice of heaven. Jarvis felt a poem coming on. He uncapped his pen, then searched his pockets for a piece of paper, finding none. He had to have paper, and soon, or the moment would be lost.

"Do you have any paper?" he asked.

"Paper?"

Jarvis nodded. Danuta handed him the Polish language newspaper. Jarvis mimed writing with his pen. "Paper," he repeated.

Danuta went to the refrigerator and tore a sheet off her magnetic memo pad, "Things to Do Today." The sheet was blank. She handed it to Jarvis.

Jarvis sat on the sofa and quickly started to pen some lines. Danuta stood watching him. She figured maybe he was a precinct captain, after all.

Danuta sat in the rocking chair by the window and watched Jarvis, who was writing so fast that his hands were leaving water marks on the paper. He writes like someone who has something to say, she thought. Maybe he is not a precinct captain.

Jarvis came to and realized he was sitting on something. He pulled a book out from under him and held it up.

"One of my favorites," he said.

"Yes?"

"The owl and the pussycat . . ."

". . . went to sea," Danuta said, completing the line.

"Your child's book?"

"And mine. I try to learn English."

"Are you in school?"

She shook her head. "I learn here."

"Is your husband teaching you?"

"My husband working. Much working."

* * * * *

Project, that was it. Project your desire. See it in your mind, pretend it's a ball, and hurl it out into the universe. Nothing like learning under pressure, thought Tyler. Okay, here goes. He saw it, he felt it, he made it into a ball, and he hurled it, not into the universe, but right at Leszek.

Suddenly, Leszek's hands stopped their trajectory, made a U-turn, and worked their way toward the glowing health of his own apple cheeks. He punched himself in the eyes, beat himself in the neck, cut a gash in his own lip.

* * * * *

"My name is Barbara," Danuta said. In Poland, Danuta had learned about America by watching *The Big Valley*. She told herself that if she ever moved to America, she would name herself after Barbara Stanwyk, a strong woman who took no nonsense from nobody no how.

"Barbara, I am Jarvis. I am an old man who has lived a long time. A year ago, I was spewed from the belly of the beast, and I have washed ashore with a new lease on life. I have made a vow to do good. To help others."

Jarvis had lost Danuta after the part about being an old man. But she could tell that he was saying something important. His white, droopy eyebrows curled upward like exclamation points. She nodded and leaned forward in her rocking chair.

". . . and so, Barbara, I am going to teach you English."

"You?"

"Yes!"

"You speak Polish?"

"No."

"How?"

"We will pray to the Holy Spirit. You have heard, perhaps, of Pentecost?"

* * * * *

Leszek thought he was dreaming and tried to wake up. But he tasted his blood and knew he was awake. I'm going crazy, he thought. Crazy, just like Uncle Roman when he sawed off his toes because his shoes were too small. If only those goddamned Care Package people had let Uncle Roman exchange the shoes—the first pair he'd had in years. But, no, they drove him crazy, and now here I am in this mini-mart, beating myself up and I can't stop.

For his part, Tyler was amazed. Jesus, Mary, and Joseph, he thought. I'm really onto something here.

CHAPTER 3

Who Wrote the Book of Love?

WHVN-FM continued to fall in the ratings; the classic lite and New Age stations were gobbling them up. The powers-that-be blamed Henry for the station's plummet to the basement. He was old; he made the entire station seem old and tired. Why, they asked him, didn't he just gracefully retire? Why didn't he accept their offer of a huge send-off to pasture?

Despite his other interests, endeavors, and sources of income, Henry did not want to lose his program. After a careful (he believed) analysis, he concluded that he was not to blame for the station's problems. There had to be other reasons for the decline. In Henry's mind, the matter became increasingly connected to the plight of Sacred Heart church.

Henry started to make some notes for a book on the subject:

In the metropolitan Chicago area, total radio listenership is up. People listen while commuting, while getting ready for work in the morning, while falling asleep at night. People listen on the job, while cooking, cleaning, taking a bath, and making love.

People listen to talk shows, ethnic programs, easy listening, new age, rock, soft rock, lite rock, classic rock, hard rock, heavy metal, rap, blues, rhythm and blues, soul, punk, new wave, oldies, gospel, country, country and western, jazz, jazz fusion, acid jazz, spirituals—and, fewer and fewer, to classical.

As the twentieth century comes to an end, radio, like religion, is a vertical medium—something for everyone. In the old days, when there were only a few radio stations, when radio was a horizontal, blanket medium—those were the days when the radio sat imposing and godlike in the family's living room. Those were the days when the plight of Little Orphan Annie or Fibber McGee and Molly commanded the attention of everyone in America. Now there are more choices.

In the old days, when Catholicism was the horizontal, blanket religion—those were the days when a church sat imposing and Godlike in a community. Those were the days when the Mass and the sacraments commanded the attention of the populace. Now there are more choices.

Even the last bastions of the faith—the Latino, Polish, and Slavic communities—are being pulled away by the charismatic promises of Pentecostalism, by the civic pride and impressive singing of Mormonism, by the wonders of Seventh Day Adventism, by the apocalyptic threats of the Jehovah's Witnesses, by the born-again certainty of the Assemblies of God. People want more from religion and from radio. Meanwhile, the pie gets sliced into smaller and smaller pieces.

The downside is dial switching. The downside is lack of history. The downside is shallow roots. Thus, today's radio stations and religions have to be constantly vigilant to keep their listeners, to retain their members. Gone are the days when listenership and church membership were givens. Gone are the days when, because these things were constant, radio stations could concentrate on programming and churches could concentrate on spirituality. Now, it's ratings. Now, it's advertising. Now, it's keeping what you have, not slipping. The medium exists to feed itself.

In his mind, Henry knew he should just bow out; but his heart would have none of it. He loved his job, he loved his program, he loved the Voice of Heaven. And he didn't want to let them go.

These days, Henry's head and his heart weren't on good terms. In this dilemma, Henry was more fortunate than most. He could work it out on paper, try to look at both sides of the issue, see if he could make some sense of it. He'd make the war between his mind and his heart a counterpoint in his book about radio and religion, the one he was going to call *Mixed Messages*—a handy title that would cover both themes.

Fine, Henry was writing a book. Henry was in control again. He had made his suffering the grist for his old mill. He had separated himself from his suffering, so that now it was as if it were all happening to someone else.

Henry was aware of what he was doing. He was avoiding suffering, albeit in a socially acceptable, perhaps even laudable way —surely, there were many who could benefit from the scholarly dissection of the issues that would be raised in the book. But despite the noble patina of Henry's motives, in his heart of hearts and in his mind of minds, he knew he was missing an opportunity.

Henry, with his deep compassion for the underclass, for the poor, for the downtrodden, for the uneducated, even for the criminal—Henry in his heart of hearts and in his mind of minds knew this was so because, deep down, he envied these people. Envied their direct experience, envied their simplicity, envied their awe, their wonder, their pain. He envied their ability to suffer, whether nobly or ignobly. This was a capacity that Henry felt was outside the realm of the intellectual, beyond the ken of the educated. The poor man suffers. The rich man becomes neurotic. Thus saith the Henry.

Rather than suffer, Henry worked. While he worked, Henry knew that he was avoiding suffering. But he rationalized: "If I stop working, I still won't be able to suffer, so I may as well work. That is, unless I take up heavy drinking."

At the end of the twentieth century, man has forgotten how to suffer. As he moves farther from his history and his God, he forgets how to be awed, moved, swept away. He believes he is the center of the universe. He believes he matters in the grand scheme of things. He believes things should always go according to plan—his. He forgets he is a speck on God's sleeve, about to be swept off into the void. He forgets that he will die.

Henry could write about anything. About his warring head and heart. About his inability to suffer. About the decline of classical music, about the splintering of religion. He could talk, talk, talk and write, write, write. He was a twentieth-century man. He was a communicator. He could talk and write about living, about life, about problems, about suffering, about pain and joy and love and religion and God and even death. But how could he ever experience these things directly?

How could he ever be truly human?

CHAPTER 4
Saint Blaise's Day

Julio needed to pray, but it was impossible now that the church had received its death sentence. No matter how hard he tried, Julio's entreaties did not rise to heaven.

He thought that if he could save Sacred Heart church, he would once again have a place to pray. So, Julio placed cardboard tubes with slotted metal tops in all the neighborhood stores—but it takes a lot of spare change to add up to a million dollars.

He visited his brujo, Manuel, and had him work a spell. But Julio felt no different after the ritual of roses and holy water.

Just this morning, the priest had blessed Julio's throat with crossed candles. Julio hoped the blessing would keep the knives away.

* * * * *

Henry Purcell ambled up the sidewalk, making his approach to WHVN. Henry had never been afraid to walk the neighborhood, any time of the day or night. He didn't expect to be bothered and he wasn't, except by the winos, who knew him as an easy mark. But, as he saw Julio jogging toward him, Henry became aware that he was alone on the street and that a young man in gang colors was fast approaching. He got out his key and moved quickly to the heavy brass door of WHVN.

"Henry," Julio called. "Hey, Enrique!"

Henry slid his key in the lock.

"Henry Purcell!"

Henry turned. Julio loomed over him in the shadow of the doorway.

"Henry Purcell," Julio repeated.

"That's what they call me."

"I need to talk to you."

"Got a show to do right now, son."

"I'll wait."

"It's gonna be a couple hours."

"I got time."

A cold shadow fell over the two men. Someone had joined them in the dark doorway. Henry turned. The new arrival took a step backward and stood in the glare of the sodium vapor streetlight. Julio and Henry jumped.

"And I thought I was looking good for myself," said Jarvis, the former judge who was to be Henry's guest on the program.

Henry laughed. "It's these goddamned streetlights. They'd make Errol Flynn look like Peter Lorre."

Though he was less than half the age of either Jarvis or Henry, Julio knew the old-time movie stars that Henry mentioned. This made Julio feel intelligent, able to hold his own in a sophisticated conversation. Julio started to hum the tune that Peter Lorre whistled in the movie *M*. Henry and Jarvis turned and looked at Julio as if he were a criminal. Julio immediately realized his mistake. A stranger in gang colors should never try to be witty.

Henry took Jarvis by the elbow and led him to the door of WHVN. "Come on," Henry said, "we've got a half hour to go over the format."

* * * * *

As a Circuit Court judge, Jarvis's courtroom was always backed up because he insisted on eliciting every conceivable detail of a case. Even after Jarvis had listened to every last "he said" and "she said" and "he did" or "she did," the Judge agonized over his decision as if he were Saint Peter at heaven's gate.

The cops and lawyers groaned when they pulled his courtroom. They knew it meant hours upon hours of listening to endless minutiae: what the defendant had for breakfast on the day of the crime, the remarks noted on grammar school report cards, whether he'd been an altar boy, what kind of music he or she listened to, their favorite sports, and on and on, ad nauseam.

During Judge Ray Jarvis's bribery trial, the lawyers who had turned state's evidence said they'd bribed the Judge as a means of preserving their livelihoods—they were going broke spending so much time in Jarvis's courtroom, and needed to find a way to speed things up.

* * * * *

Henry opened the door, and Julio followed.

"Son, I've got work to do right now."

"I'll wait. I have to talk to you."

"What about?"

"I want to get out of the gang."

Jarvis started to have flashbacks. He was back on the bench, and this young punk was begging for another chance.

Henry sighed. He had a heart problem, emotionally speaking. "Come on," he finally said.

Julio followed his two old guides into the hallowed halls of WHVN-FM, the voice of heaven. He was inside! Finally inside WHVN, the mysterious seat of culture and sophistication. He had grown up in the shadow of the station's red and white tower. As a child, he had imagined climbing that tower all the way to heaven.

As they made their way through the dim offices, Julio breathed deeply, as if he were in a high altitude where the air was thin. In the semi-darkness, he felt his way forward, feeling the back of a chair, the edge of a desk. Ahead of him, the white heads of Henry and Jarvis lit the way.

They traveled through a dark corridor, where there were no landmarks, and the heads of Julio's companions had faded into halos. Julio half-expected to see phantoms jump out of the darkness.

* * * * *

All his life Julio had encountered ghosts. When he was small, there was a ghost that folded itself up and slid into his right shoe each night. When he was five, the ghost of George Washington, whom he later recognized on a dollar bill, had stood before him and pushed his swing in the playground, as his mother pushed from behind. The ghosts, the visions, became part of the scenery of his life. In grammar school, the nuns were surprised that Julio had no trouble grasping the most abstract of concepts—the Holy Ghost.

* * * * *

A door opened and light flooded over him. Julio followed his two old guides into the room.

"Sit here," Henry said, indicating a chair. "You can watch us through the window."

Julio watched as Henry and Jarvis entered the windowed room and took their places at a table equipped with microphones. Henry flipped a switch and Julio could hear his voice.

"Do you want to listen?"

Julio nodded.

"I just want to talk to the Judge for a minute, and when we're ready to go on, I'll tune you in."

* * * * *

The Judge would not have been tempted except for the twins. His son aspired to Ivy League schools and lakefront condos. His daughter had set her sights on an equestrian career. Each day as he arrived home weary from court, they wouldn't even wait until he'd removed his hat before they began their litany of requests.

Their mother had died several years before, and Jarvis felt he needed to do what he could to salve the wound. So, when Al Gardner made his first tentative proposal—two round trip tickets to Florida that he couldn't use, and could the Judge do something with them?—Jarvis agreed. Word got around, and soon the Judge was receiving offers on a daily basis.

When the ax finally fell—part of a major undercover operation looking for corruption in the city's government—it was almost a relief. Even jail seemed a respite from his children's unceasing demands.

* * * * *

Julio wondered why no one else was at the station. He knew that WHVN broadcast 24 hours a day. They must prerecord some stuff, he thought. The music plays all by itself.

As a child, Julio believed that angels worked at the station ceaselessly, night and day and holidays, spinning records of sublime music. Sometimes, the angels even sang. Whenever he wanted his mother to turn on the station, he'd say: "Angel music," and she immediately knew what he meant. But now Julio was here and there were no angels. There was no one except himself and the two ancients.

He watched as Henry and Jarvis moved their lips and gestured to each other across the table. They appeared to be in a heated discussion. It was like watching a silent movie, except there were no placards telling you what was going on. There was no organist lending drama to the movements. Just two sentimental, old, non-macho men flapping their jaws in silence.

"Good evening, night owls. This is Henry Purcell, the voice of reason in an unreasoning world. Tonight, I have as my guest Raymond L. Jarvis, former Circuit Court judge—and one of those convicted in the government's Operation Bloodhound probe. The Judge has served his debt to society, and has joined us tonight to share his perspectives on a variety of subjects. So, stay tuned."

Julio watched as Henry pressed a button.

A mellow voice said: *You are listening to WHVN, the voice of heaven on your FM dial.*

Henry moved up to the edge of his chair as he anticipated the end of the announcement. He was in his working stance: alert, ready.

"Judge Jarvis . . ."

"Just Jarvis, if you will, Henry."

"Jarvis, do you harbor any bitterness toward those who sent you away?"

"None whatsoever, Henry."

"You mean, you don't even bear a scintilla of a grudge?"

"Not a trace of one."

"But how can that be? One day, you're on top of the world. You're like Solomon, meting out justice. The next day, you're in the slammer servin' time."

"It was the best thing that ever happened to me, Henry. I got out of the rat race, away from the stress, the pressure. Now, I have nothing to prove. I can live as I please."

"And what pleases you, Jarvis?"

"Well, Henry, I'm teaching reading to non-English speaking immigrants, and I'm writing poetry. I'm raising money to repair Sacred Heart church, and I'm taking petitions around to get you back on at your regular . . . ."

Henry, who knew that the station management was looking for the slimmest reason to give him the boot, pressed the button.

You are listening to WHVN, the voice of heaven on your FM dial. Julio could see Henry waving his finger at Jarvis as he continued to press the button with his other hand. *You are listening to WHVN, the voice of heaven on your FM dial.* With one hand still on the button, Henry opened the door and ordered Jarvis to get out. Jarvis, who, since the time he'd been "spewed from the belly of the beast," was unshakable, took it in stride and left with dignity.

As Jarvis was making his way out, Henry waved Julio into the room. Julio looked around, figuring maybe one of the angels had appeared, after all. But no one else was there. Henry must be waving to me, he thought.

* * * * *

His doctor had recommended an early release. Jarvis needed a coronary bypass. And so he was out. Just like that. Swept away in a screaming ambulance and deposited in the halls of St. Francis Hospital.

As they were wheeling him up to surgery, Jarvis had a vision of his heart as a giant helium-filled float in a Thanksgiving Day parade. High in the air, held by strings from the ground, his heart strained to pull away, to rise high above the city and hover there for all to see and point at. "There," they would say, "it's the Judge's heart. See how big it is, how red, like a Valentine from God." Then angels playing harps would appear, forming a halo around his heart. His heart would beat and throb, keeping time to their heavenly music.

As the attendants wheeled him through the hospital corridors, Jarvis was far away, smiling, and thinking about his heart with awe.

* * * * *

Julio entered the studio and sat at the table. Henry closed the door and took his hand off the button.

"I have as my guest tonight a young lad from the streets. This young lad, who will have to remain anonymous, desires to quit his gang."

Henry pressed the button.

You are listening to WHVN, the voice of heaven on your FM dial.

While the announcement played repeatedly, Henry managed to convince Julio not to jump out of his chair and follow in Jarvis's still-warm footsteps.

"We'll have to call you something. Pick a name. Any name."

This was a golden opportunity for Julio. He could rename himself. Quickly, his mind scanned all of his favorite rock stars and movie heroes, then leaped over to the saints and the angels of the church.

"Gabriel," he said.

The announcement stopped.

"We'll call our guest Gabriel, though that's not his real name. This young gent has grown up on the streets of this city and, like many young lads, has had to learn how to survive on those streets. For many of our youth, survival means gang membership. But what if you want *out*? Let's talk to our guest."

Henry motioned for Julio to move closer to the table. Julio scooted forward and looked uneasily at the microphone, as if it were a conjurer's wand.

"So, Gabe, how long you been in the gang?"

"Ten years."

"Ten years?"

"Yes, ten years."

"An entire decade, huh?"

"Yes, if you want to put it that way."

"You have been in the gang for a tenth of a century, is that right?"

Julio felt like he was back in math class.

"It has been a long time," he replied, hoping Henry would shift to another subject. He had never liked numbers.

"So, Gabe, you have been in the gang for many years."

"That's right."

"And now you want out."

"Yes." Julio hoped his mother was in bed asleep. He hoped she did not have her frequent insomnia and was not tuned in right now.

"Could you tell us why?"

"I want to do other things."

"Please share them with us, Gabe."

"I want to get a good job and move away from the neighborhood."

"Why don't you just get a good job and stay in the neighborhood?"

"Because then I would have to stay in the gang."

"And what do you do in the gang?"

"Do?"

"What is the purpose of the gang?"

"Purpose?"

"Are you engaged in any criminal activities?"

"No. No. Of course not."

"We have guaranteed your anonymity. You can come clean with us, Gabe."

"We protect the neighborhood, that's all."

"So, this gang of yours is nothing more than a band of protecting angels, sent down to guard the teeming masses?"

"I wouldn't put it like that," said Julio, though in his heart of hearts, that's just how he'd put it.

"You mean to tell me your gang is not involved in drugs or violence?"

"We protect the neighborhood."

"By warring with rival gangs, protecting your turf?"

"Protection takes many forms," said Julio, wishing Henry would go back to the arithmetic questions.

"So, how do you quit a gang when you've had enough? Tell us, Gabriel."

"That's what I was hoping you could tell me."

"Me? Why me?"

"Because you are old and you seem to know things."

Henry, indeed, was old. But he didn't like to be reminded of it. He had always looked old and wise, even when he'd been forty. He was now over seventy, and looked better than most of his cronies. Ah, he thought, when you're twenty you can't appreciate a well-preserved senior citizen when you see one.

"Well, Gabriel, how about tryin' to reason with your cohorts? Be straight with 'em. Tell 'em you want out."

I should have known better, thought Julio.

"But, of course, that won't work," said Henry, thinking out loud. "No, you need to do something more convincing, more dramatic."

"Yes," Julio replied. "Do you have any ideas?"

CHAPTER 5

The Letter of the Law

It had started as a way to pass the time while traveling to and from work. Norma's daily commute was the worst part of her day. The crowded trains and buses meant she had to stand for nearly an hour, pushed and jostled by unwashed, uncouth, unshaven, unruly fellow passengers.

Squeezed in, it was difficult to read even the tabloid-sized *Sun-Times*. And, even when God smiled and she *did* manage to get a miracle of a seat, the bumping, bouncing, rocking, and rolling of the train or bus made Norma feel nauseous when her eyes scanned a line of type. Letter writing was out, as well. More than once, when the subway had screeched to a stop, Norma's pen had inched its way beyond the paper and onto her coat or skirt.

In her zeal not to waste time, Norma had even tried to do a needlepoint of Nuestra Señora de Guadalupe appearing to Juan Diego—and had narrowly missed putting out her seat partner's eye as she pulled up the embroidery needle while the subway was slamming to a halt. For a few days, Norma had borrowed Julio's Walkman and listened to WHVN, but had given it up when she got so caught up in the music that she missed her stop for two days straight.

What was left? Well, there were always prayers. There was always the rosary. But, as was her habit since youth, Norma frequently caught herself moving her lips while praying. This would not have bothered Norma—who cared, anyway, about a bus or train full of mostly uncivilized strangers?—had she not looked up during a particularly animated recitation of the Apostle's Creed and spotted the scornful face of Millie Kimball, the boss's trouble-making secretary.

No, obviously Norma would have to think of something else. But what? Reading was making her seasick. Writing was running up her cleaning bill. Needlepoint could land her in jail. The radio was causing her to be late. Praying was jeopardizing her job.

One day in desperation, Norma stared up at an advertisement and blankly began to pick out the letters of the alphabet. *Pregnant, unwed, in distress? We want to help. Call this toll-free number.* A, no b, c, d, e, f, g, h, i, no j, no k, l, m, n, o, p, no q, r, s, t, u, no v, w, no x, no y, no z. Norma moved up the aisle, repeating this process with every ad, until it was time to get off the train.

Norma did this for several days running, until the idea came to her that she could think of a psalm, song, poem, or passage from the Bible and try to pick it out of the ads.

Norma was excited when she got on the "L" the first day she hit on this idea. It would be fun, a challenge, a game. Something to occupy her mind and keep her from the idleness she so dreaded. For her first attempt, Norma selected John 1:1, "In the beginning was the Word, and the Word was with God and the Word was God."

* * * * *

Manuel was about to close up shop for the afternoon. He'd just eaten a large meal at Sophie's Restaurant, a warm, homey place that was clean and bright and the Polish food was always good and plentiful. Manuel could feel the full weight of the potato pancakes, the sour cream, and the pierogis on his stomach. He wished he could go home for a short rest, but he was booked up and needed to hurry. The bad spirits never rested and neither could he.

There was the house cleansing on Honore Street, the man with the melting face over on Armitage, and, of course, there was always Emilia, the child who ate dirt. There was always so much work and so little time. Manuel sighed. If only he could find an apprentice to help with the load.

Manuel was picking up his keys when Leszek pushed through the door, making the botanica's tiny welcome bell sound like the call for a five-alarm fire.

"You are Manuel," Leszek panted out through his short breaths.

"I am busy," Manuel said.

"You must help me," Leszek demanded.

"If you will make an appointment . . ." began Manuel.

"Someone has put a curse on me," Leszek screamed.

* * * * *

Despite her Catholicism, Norma read daily from an oversized white leatherette King James version of the Bible. She'd purchased it from a door-to-door salesman, whose photo she later saw in the post office as a criminal wanted for selling pornography through the mails. By that time, Norma had already formed a deep attachment to the Bible, and had carefully inscribed all the births and deaths and marriages of her family in its opening pages. The salesman had been a scoundrel, yet Norma continued to find the Bible, and its poetic language, comforting—even though it wasn't an official Catholic version.

Norma was beaming as she walked up the bus steps. At last, something useful to do during this empty time! Norma's idle hours of daily commuting had left her with a deep empathy for the Israelites who had wandered forty years in the desert. But no more. Now, I have a mission, Norma thought. I will make some sense out of the senselessness. And I will begin with the Gospel according to John.

* * * * *

"Sir, you are not alone. There are many who share your bad fortune. Right now, there are three urgent cases that I must attend to." Manuel moved toward the door, but Leszek stood in his path.

"My coworker, Carlos Flores, sent me," said Leszek, hoping he would incur some special privilege by invoking a compatriot's name.

"Carlos should have told you that you would need an appointment. Would you appear at your doctor's office and demand immediate attention?"

"If I am dying, yes."

"And are you dying now?"

"My soul has been shot with a poison arrow. You must pull it out and show me how to get my revenge."

"Do I know you?"

"I don't know."

"Yes, I remember. Your band played at Sophie's daughter's wedding."

"Yes, yes, that was me."

"And I have seen you at Sacred Heart. You have a little daughter and a pretty wife."

Pretty wife! Did every man in this country feel free to comment on his wife's looks? What kind of unspeakable thoughts was Danuta inspiring in these men? No, she would never go to work, even if she *did* learn English.

"Yes," was all that Leszek replied.

Manuel opened a drawer and pulled out his large, black appointment book. He scanned the coming week. "I could see you on Tuesday at five," he said.

"No, you must help me now!" Leszek started to weep and covered his face with his hands. Manuel helped him to a chair. He sighed. Every doctor had his emergencies. The others would have to wait.

* * * * *

The first ad Norma approached was an old standby that had been appearing on public transportation for more than ten years. The ad appealed to people who had to stand for long periods on moving trains and buses. *Corns? Calluses? Bunions? Athlete's foot? Heel pain? Ingrown toenails? Hammer toes? Warts? We'll get you back on your feet. Call today.* It was all there. Every last letter of John 1:1. The entire quotation on her very first try.

Norma was elated. Imagine, finding God's word amid the mammon of worldly advertisements! Since she had experienced beginner's luck at the very start of her commute, Norma was left with forty minutes to fill. There was still the rest of the elevated ride, the subway, and the entire bus ride to think about. Perhaps she should try another quotation on a different ad.

But what? Something from the Old Testament? Unbidden, a verse popped into Norma's mind. What a strange verse to think of, she told herself. *Ye are gods and all ye are children of the most high.*

* * * * *

Leszek sat staring off into the distance, arms hanging limply at his sides, as he told of his encounter with Tyler at the mini-mart. Manuel listened silently.

When he was finished, Leszek gazed into Manuel's face. Manuel looked into Leszek's eyes only long enough to register the man's utter desolation. He began to pace the room. Leszek, who had an immigrant's respect for real estate, was concerned that Manuel's fast pacing would wear a groove right into the floor.

"We will need to know his name," Manuel finally announced.

"His name is Tyler. T-Y-L-E-R. It is on his shirt."

Manuel smiled. It is always easier to find out the name of a blue-collar worker. The nature of their work makes them easy targets.

"So, you will help me?"

"I will do what I can."

"How much will I need to pay you?"

Manuel's business operated on a sliding scale. In this way, he was like the Catholic Church. You paid what you could afford.

He looked at the man seated before him and saw a perfect specimen of the hard-working Pole who knew how to save money to buy real estate. Manuel figured the man had thousands socked away. There were not many like him who came Manuel's way.

Manuel closed his eyes to seek the counsel of his inner voice. "How much should I charge him?" Manuel said silently to the voice that guided him.

"Nothing," replied the voice.

"Nothing?" Manuel responded incredulously. "But this guy is loaded."

"Yes," said the voice.

"Then why?" entreated Manuel.

"Because," said the voice, "you have found your apprentice."

* * * * *

Norma started to pick out the verse from an ad next to the bus's rear exit. The illustration showed the classic drawing of a Victorian woman viewing herself in a mirror. Depending on how you looked at it, the drawing showed either a beautiful woman or a skull. The ad copy read: "Drugs may seem beautiful at first, but sooner or later they'll kill you. If you need help, call now." It was all there. Double beginner's luck. Or was it? Could it be that no matter which verse came to Norma, she would find just the ad to give it life? This was an astounding thought. Just what was at work here? Just what had she hit upon?

And it came to pass that whatever Bible verse entered Norma's mind, there was an ad right there to sing its praises to the world. Knowing in advance that she would find what she was looking for took the challenge out of it. But, over the course of weeks, the undertaking had evolved from an amusement to a mission.

Norma believed that she was helping to cure all the ills of society that were neatly encapsulated in the ads displayed on public transportation. AIDS, drugs, unwanted pregnancies, homelessness, poverty, all varieties of disease—even hammer toes.

But, like any zealot, even Christ Himself, perhaps even the unflappable Sister Merlina Talbott, Norma became overwhelmed with the burden of her mission. The weight of the world seemed to press on Norma during her daily commutes.

* * * * *

Manuel turned his horrified face to Leszek, who had been watching Manuel's silent communion with the higher power. Leszek jumped up, thinking Manuel had detected a rat under his chair.

"What is it?" asked Leszek.

"The spirit says that it has sent you to be my apprentice."

"Me? No!"

"You. Yes. The spirit never lies."

"But I am already working three jobs!"

"You will have to somehow find the time. Perhaps your wife will need to seek employment."

It always came back to this. His wife. It was the remark about his wife that had started all this, that had led him here, and now she would have to find a job, and men would feast their eyes on her to their hearts' content.

"My wife will never work!"

"A pretty woman can always find a job," said Manuel. "Right now, Sophie is looking for a waitress."

"My wife will never be a waitress. She is an educated woman. A nurse."

"Then send her to work in a hospital. Nurses are always needed."

"She does not speak English."

"Then send her to WHVN. Sophie tells me they are looking for someone to host the Great Polish Composers program."

"WHVN! Never! It haunts my life! Their music plays in my house night and day and I have no radio!"

"The spirit has told me that you are to be my apprentice. It is not as I would have wished, either, my friend. But we have no say in these things. Come. We must get started."

"Started?"

"You are to accompany me on my visits today."

"I am working tonight. I need to go home and tune my guitar and replace a string."

"You will be back in time," said Manuel as he opened the door and led Leszek into the bright daylight of a fourth job and a new career.

* * * * *

Looking back on her days of idle innocence, Norma was sometimes overwhelmed with nostalgia. How simple life was then. How uncomplicated by duty. How vast the possibilities. But now her life had tunneled into a hard, narrow line: finding the word of God in carnal advertising verbiage. If she neglected this duty, Norma felt the world would suffer some terrible fate—a nuclear war, a decimating plague, famine, pestilence. Whenever Norma pondered her mission, she had a mental image of Moses delivering the Israelites out of Egypt. She knew she had a similar task.

The work was taking its toll. Norma had always kept up her looks and, at forty-five, looked ten years younger. But the intense concentration and daily dedication required by her mission had caused the already slim Norma to lose ten pounds. Most of the weight seemed to come off of her face. Her formerly smooth, unlined skin grew loose. The area under her eyes grew puffy. She grew pale. Once, when she was trying on a pair of shoes, she looked up into the mirror and was shocked to see that her entire face looked as if it were being pulled by a vacuum.

Norma had no energy left for anything but her task. Even Julio's pronouncement that he intended to quit the gang—an answer to many years of prayers—had no effect on Norma. When Julio told her the news, all she could manage was a weak smile and a nod. She was feeling increasingly detached from her personal cares. She now had a larger venue: the world, which she was now responsible for saving.

No wonder, Norma thought, no wonder people do not want to do God's work. It is too much. The burden is too heavy, no matter what the Bible says. How did I stumble on this work? I, a silly woman, thought that I could amuse myself at God's expense. And here I am now, a slave to God. No life of my own anymore. I am growing old. I am growing distant from my family. Please, God, deliver me. Deliver me!

In her despair, Norma looked for relief from the burden that was consuming her life. She could try not to do it for a day and test the waters—see if a calamity resulted from her neglect. She could perform the task every other day and see if God would still be appeased. She could try to unload the job on someone else—some poor bag lady who lived on public transportation anyway. Norma could quit her job, get something within walking distance, so she no longer had to ride buses and "L's." Even God would understand that she could not do the work if her job no longer required that she ride public transportation.

Though Norma almost convinced herself, she knew that her rationalizations would not hold water with God. She would have to find a way out—yet in a manner that would appease, even please, the Almighty.

As had often happened since her encounter with Sister Merlina Talbott, Norma's mind once again glided over the events of that evening. Certainly, it had been one of the most striking experiences of Norma's life. But why was she thinking about it now, when she was trying to find an answer to this particular dilemma? Perhaps Norma's discontent was God's way of showing her what she must do. Norma had a calling, and had discovered a new way of worshipping God.

Norma Villalobos was about to found a new religion.

CHAPTER 6

Ave Maria

If his plan worked, Julio would be free to become *un bombero*, a fireman who could climb the high ladder as he had imagined climbing WHVN's tower as a child. If the plan did not work, he would be dead, and he hoped it would be quick and painless.

It was Saturday night. During the week, Julio had spread the word that there would be a new spot for the meeting—Sacred Heart. Julio had obtained a key from one of the stalwarts of the church, a man named Stanislaw who couldn't do enough for Julio, ever since the gang leader had saved his little daughter from slipping onto the elevated tracks. Lucky thing, to have people who owed you favors, especially this time, Julio thought. He would be spared the indignity of having to pick the church's massive lock.

Julio had thought long and hard to figure a way out of the gang. He needed a plan with drama, with style. And he believed he had hit on just the thing. The doomed church was the only place that would suit his purposes. He needed just the right atmosphere for the pronouncement he was about to make.

Julio arrived at the church an hour before the midnight meeting. He inserted the huge brass skeleton key in the lock, turned it, and listened as the tumbler turned with a fateful thunk.

In the darkness, he felt for the holy water, crossed himself, genuflected, then moved slowly down the center aisle toward the altar. All around, candles flickered in blue and red glass holders. Julio looked up at the stained glass windows. There, in each one, images of the Lord's sacred, thorny heart were lit up by the streetlights outside. As Julio walked down the center aisle, he saw the shadows of God's heart everywhere—on the pews, on the walls, on the floor. He was careful where he stepped.

His high-heeled boots hit the floor, step after slow step, the sound careening off the walls and up to the church's high dome. The colored glass, the scent of burning beeswax, the shadowy statues of Jesus and Mary and Angels and Saints—all the things that made the church such a comfort during a crowded daytime Mass—now made Julio's heart lurch in fear.

He knelt in the front pew, bowed his head, and prayed for God and the Angels and Saints, and, most of all, the Blessed Virgin, to understand why he must do what he was about to do.

* * * * *

For weeks, Esperanza had been tormented by strange dreams and fantasies and had called out repeatedly for mercy. Her prayers to the Virgin of Guadalupe remained unanswered.

It was just past midnight, the first hours of a Sunday morning. Esperanza's feet were leading her to Sacred Heart, yet her mind told her the church would be locked tight. The three-block walk to Sacred Heart was a continual war between Esperanza's two selves. She'd take a step, and her foot would stop in mid-air. "Turn around. Go home," her rational voice would say. But before she could retrace even one step, her intuition would tell her: "Keep going. Don't stop." With her constant stopping and starting, by the time she arrived at the church's crumbling stone steps, she felt as if she had just completed a grueling bout of calisthenics.

Sacred Heart's famous marble angels stood sentry on both sides of each step. Some of the angels held trumpets to their lips, others held small harps or lutes. How the angels must love music, Esperanza thought. And with this thought, her mind filled with the most heavenly music she had ever heard. Sweet high voices. Sublime sounds. Angel music. The sheer perfection of it made her start to weep. I can die now, she thought, and the music abruptly stopped. From now on, she told herself, I must learn to still my thoughts.

* * * * *

Julio heard the door creak open behind him, then footsteps coming closer. Jaime and Alberto nodded to him and sat in the pews across the aisle. Then the door creaked open again and again. Julio felt bodies filling up the pews behind him. Quiet talking, murmurs. They could have been reciting the rosary.

Julio did not have to turn around and look. A solid feeling in his diaphragm told him that everyone was there. He rose slowly from his seat. The murmuring suddenly stopped, as if it were a sound effect that had been abruptly cut off. All eyes were on the back of Julio's leather jacket.

Julio walked up the steps to the altar, then turned to face the crowd that sat at attention before him.

"Compadres," he said, his voice hollow and tinny. He had hoped this would not happen. He had hoped that his voice would not betray him. Now he needed a solid voice, a full basso, a voice that would shake the very rafters and leave a shower of roof tiles on the street below. But his voice was thin, unmanly, like that recording he had heard in history class of Franklin Roosevelt, all high and whiny and Julio had wondered how anyone could have ever called the man a great leader. A leader must have a powerful voice. Julio needed a room full of bodies to absorb his sounds and play them back to him, to return his voice in its richness and fullness. But there was no retreating. He needed to go on, despite the cartoon voice that was causing him such shame, such pain.

"I have called you here tonight to tell you that I must step down as your leader, that I must leave the only family I have known."

Before Julio could continue, raucous laughter broke out among the crowd. Julio, always the joker. Calling them here to this spooky place to pull a stunt. So that's what this was all about, they thought. En mass, the crowd relaxed, elbowed each other, smiled, bent over and slapped their knees, smoothed hair, felt for their wallets, and performed all the other ritualistic behavior that heralds a return to normalcy.

Julio held up his hands and shook his head.

"No, brothers, it is not as you think. I am speaking the truth. I am leaving because . . ." He stopped, then turned and looked to the painting of The Virgin of Guadalupe. "Because I have had a vision of the Virgin. She has told me I must leave the Latin Lords and do some service for her. I must do as she says. I have no . . . ."

Even though Julio had carefully prepared his speech and had practiced it many times before the bathroom mirror, the rest of his words flew from his mind. He was speechless, struck dumb by the sight that now presented itself to his bulging eyes.

For at that very moment, down the center aisle came a woman wearing a long pink dress and a blue hooded cape. Her head was bowed and her hands were folded.

The gang members turned to see what had captured Julio's attention. It took only one brief glance. In an instant, the crowd was on its knees, heads bowed, hands folded, eyes closed, shoulders shaking.

The lady made her way up to the front pew, genuflected, then knelt and started to say a rosary.

* * * * *

Julio could only move his eyes, which darted from the painting of The Virgin of Guadalupe to the one who sat in the front pew. The same dress, the same blue cape, the same beatific expression.

Serves me right, Julio thought in the midst of his frozen pain. Serves me right. I thought I could use God's mother as an excuse.

But in an instant Julio's mind switched to another track. I can't get away with anything, he thought. I never get a break. This should have gone smoothly. It was a good plan. But, here, now, look, God's mother herself has come to mock me.

* * * * *

Esperanza crossed herself with the rosary's crucifix and began to pray the Apostles' Creed.

Creo en Dios, Padre todopoderoso, creador del cielo y de la tierra . . .

Why is that man standing up there at the altar, she thought. She caught her mind wandering and immediately went back to her task.

. . . creo en Jesucristo su unico hijo, nuestro senor, que fue concebido por obra y gracia del Espiritu Santo . . .

She turned and looked at the men sitting in the pews on the other side of the church. Why were they sweating and shaking, as if they were hot and cold at the same time? No, I must pray. I must not think.

. . . nacio de Santa Maria Virgen; padecio bajo el poder de Poncio Pilato; fue crucificado, muerto y sepultado; descendio a los iniernos . . .

Descended into hell, Esperanza thought. Yes, I know what that is like. She shook her head and held the crucifix tightly.

Al tercer dia resucito de entre los muertos; subio a los cielos y esta a la diestra de Dios Padre; desde alli ha de venir a juzgar a los vivos y a los muertos . . .

He will judge the living and the dead, so we are judged twice— here and in the hereafter. Don't think, pray, she told herself.

. . . Creo en el Espiritu Santo, en la Santa Iglesia Catolica, la communion de los Santos en el perdon de los pecados, la resurreccion de los muertos . . .

The resurrection of the dead, what would that look like? Bodies rising from graves, flying through the air. With a great effort, Esperanza stilled her mind to recite the prayer's final words.

. . . y la vida eterna. Amen.

At this rate, it would take her until morning to recite the five decades of the rosary, with its numerous "Hail Mary's," "Our Father's," and "Glory Be's."

She sighed and moved her fingers to the first bead of the rosary, and began the "Padrenuestro." But before she even got to the part about "hallowed be Thy name," the frozen man near the altar fell to his knees and started to weep and recite the "Ave Maria" in a voice that reminded Esperanza of Mickey Mouse.

"Dios te salve, Maria. Llena eres de gracia . . ." the man said through his sobs. The others quickly joined in.

". . . El Senor es contigo. Bendia tu eres entre todas las mujeres . . ."

So that's it, thought Esperanza. This is some kind of midnight prayer society. They looked at me so strangely because this is a private group and I should not be here. She rose from her kneeling position, entered the aisle, genuflected, then made her way out of the church to the final strains of the prayer.

". . . ahora y en la hora de nuestra muerte. Amen."

CHAPTER 7

More Things in Heaven and Earth

Between his job repairing heating-ventilation-and-air-conditioning equipment, his night job as a janitor, his weekend gig as a Dixieland jazzman, and his apprenticeship with Manuel, Leszek was too exhausted to keep track of his attractive wife's whereabouts.

Danuta spent most of her free time with the old man who was secretly teaching her English. Leszek knew about the lessons, but was too worn down to have a major confrontation with the two of them. Let them do as they please.

Leszek was afraid of falling asleep while driving, afraid he would be written up for napping on the job, as he had once done in a crawl space in the Sears Tower.

Leszek had always taken for granted his strong back and quick mind. But now his body and mind were becoming weaker by the day, and the feeling he'd always counted on—of commanding and ordering his life—was gone. Even his long-held dream of an immaculate six-flat apartment building held no charm for him. He was losing interest in his wife, rarely spoke to his child, and hadn't been to church in weeks.

He could have kept it all going if it had not been for the apprenticeship with Manuel. That had put him over the edge. But they had made a deal; and Leszek, despite his enervated state, still had his old-world honor. Yes, he had gotten his revenge on that inbred mini-mart clerk, Tyler. But Leszek knew he would be paying for the rest of his life.

* * * * *

Tyler was unaware that Leszek and Manuel had performed a revenge ritual on him. The ritual had taken place in the back room of Manuel's botanica. When Leszek asked what consequences Tyler could expect from the spell, Manuel merely shook his head and beamed the full width of his beautiful smile.

This broad smile was Leszek's first clue about an aspect of his mentor's personality: above all else, Manuel was a man with a sense of humor. The spell on Tyler bore this out. Manuel had a way of looking into the most secret place in someone's soul, seeing what the person wanted most in the world, and then providing it—with a twist.

* * * * *

Leszek kept going, but he knew it was only a matter of time. Each day he was careful to wear only good socks—those with no holes in the toes. He wouldn't want anyone to remove the shoes from his dead body and see his big toes sticking up in the air.

Lack of sleep, lack of food, constant activity. He started to have visions. Once, when Leszek was on his knees with his head inside a furnace, he groped for a wrench, and felt someone put the tool into his hand. He pulled his head out of the furnace and saw Saint Michael the Archangel organizing his tool box. Leszek fell to the floor.

"Forgive me," Leszek said, thinking the angel had appeared to smite him for what he had done to Tyler.

"You must keep your tools in order," replied Saint Michael.

"I'm sorry," Leszek sobbed.

"Try to keep the screws and bolts separated from the washers and the nuts," Saint Michael said as he aligned Leszek's set of Phillips-head screwdrivers.

"I will," Leszek said, and, when there was no reply, he looked up and the angel was gone.

Another time, Leszek had seen Saint Jude, with a flame over his head, dancing the bunny hop during the waning hours of a wedding reception the Dixie Dandies were playing. A good dancer, Leszek thought through his fog of fatigue.

There were other visions, as well. Saint Theresa talking to him from her framed picture in Manuel's botanica. "You're putting too much sage in the bowl. It's a potion, not turkey dressing."

Leszek did not resist these visions. He decided they were not real, but only the result of his addled brain and atrophying body. When they happened, Leszek felt as if he were in a restaurant where a TV was playing. The visions, the pictures, were there—and he could watch or not watch, as he wished.

* * * * *

After his separation from Deeanna, Tyler fell back to daydreaming about being the powerful, handsome titan who could make women swoon. His job at the mini-mart, with its abundance of reading material and steady stream of faces, helped to assuage his loneliness. But all of these new books and all of these new faces stimulated Tyler in ways he had never experienced before. He wanted more. More out of life. More from other people. *If only I were a handsome man*, he thought. *Then people would respect me, women would love me, and I could get a decent job where nobody would pick on me.*

This was the secret that Tyler harbored in the deepest part of his soul. And this was the secret that Manuel had detected, the secret that had made Manuel smile so devilishly.

* * * * *

Leszek arose every morning at 5:30, and left the house by six o'clock. He started his HVAC shift at seven, got a half hour for lunch, and clocked out at 3:30. His janitor's job in a downtown high-rise began at five, and, depending on where his day job had taken him, he either just made it or had a half hour to spare. In the latter case, he tried to get a short nap in the supply room. These brief sleeps, with their dreams of labor, often left him even more exhausted. Leszek cleaned offices from five to nine, then drove to Manuel's botanica, where he worked from 9:30 to midnight, following a list of chores that Manuel had left for him.

Sometimes, Leszek had to mop the floors with a mixture of water, salt, and rose petals. Other times he had to wash the big windows outside, or remove the candles, holy pictures, and potions from their shelves and dust. Often he had to mix potions, using an old-fashioned scale and tiny spoons to measure the many powders.

When Leszek locked the door at midnight, he drove home, where he showered and fell into bed at one a.m. If he was lucky, he would sleep for several hours. But the more exhausted he became, the harder it was to fall asleep. Usually, he was wide awake when the alarm rang.

* * * * *

Manuel and Leszek had performed the spell at midnight on the night of a full moon. At that time, Tyler was in bed asleep. The Nigel Clive book, *Key to the Meaning of Life*, lay open beside him. Ever since the incident with Leszek, Tyler had been studying the book, trying to follow its guidance—but in a more positive way. He was going to harness the power to remake himself in a more beautiful image.

* * * * *

Leszek's life had followed the same pattern for months. And this particular day promised to be the same. Leszek had had his head in many furnaces during the day, and now it was 8 p.m. and he was pushing his big trash bin from desk to desk, emptying wastebaskets.

Leszek had never been in the office during working hours, when bodies and voices and ringing telephones and the hum of machinery played themselves out there. But the energy of all this activity lingered heavily, like the memory of a lost love. He never felt more lonely than when he wove his way through the maze of unoccupied desks and chairs.

It was not merely a matter of being alone, of being the only one there. No. There had been many times back home, walking through the Bialowieza Forest, when he had been totally alone, but had never felt lonely. The forest was strange, like something from a dream, and when Leszek walked there, he felt as if he were back at the beginning of time. Sometimes, in the deep stillness, with his back against a gigantic tree, Leszek half-expected to see a dinosaur peeking its head through the top branches, half-expected to see Adam and Eve running naked through the pines. In the forest, Leszek had sometimes felt frightened, sometimes felt strange, sometimes felt so alive and opened up that the whole world seemed to be rushing in on him. But he had never, ever felt lonely.

Moving from empty office to empty office, Leszek felt like the world's last survivor walking amid the ruins. So, this was Western Civilization! Calendars and computers and telephones. Write it all down in your field notes, Leszek. You, the archaeologist, you the garbage dumper, you who picks up the pieces and cleans up the mess of the civilized world.

This was the only time Leszek had any real feelings anymore—when he was alone in the vacated office. His exhaustion had robbed him of the ability to feel pain or love or hunger or desire. All that was left was loneliness.

* * * * *

The morning after the revenge ritual, Tyler noticed that his teeth looked a little straighter when he brushed them. He noticed some new sprouts of hair growing out of his bald spot. When he put on his pants, he noticed they were a little shorter. There seemed to be more flesh on his bony cheeks. His Adam's apple didn't stick out as much. Instead of their usual dead gray, his eyes had a bright blue tinge.

Manuel (not one to miss an event with such potential for personal levity), though sleeping, projected his spirit to Tyler's rundown apartment. He watched as Tyler discovered each new facet of his emerging beauty. Manuel, unaware that Tyler had already taken the matter into his own hands, was puzzled that the man was not more surprised. When Tyler said, "It's working," Manuel was perplexed. What is working? Has this man been praying for a miracle? If so, he is about to lose his faith, Manuel thought, as his spirit rejoined his sleeping body.

* * * * *

It was now almost 8:30 at night. A few more trash cans to dump, then a quick run-through to turn off the lights. Leszek took a step into a corner office and was startled to see someone sitting with his back to him. This had never happened before. Nobody ever stayed late.

Leszek figured maybe this was the company president or some other higher-up. A man with a lot on his mind. Maybe right now he was trying to figure out how to keep the company afloat. Perhaps he was poring over documents with tiny print and obscure language, trying to make some sense of them. No, Leszek thought, I cannot intrude. Even if it means I will be written up for not dumping his trash.

As Leszek started to take a soft backward step out of the room, the man turned in his chair. The sight of the man's face made the entire surface of Leszek's skin feel like it was on fire—as if he, himself, had turned into a Callaghan furnace. When the man turned, the face Leszek saw was his own staring back at him. He was looking at his very double.

* * * * *

And then it happened. Tyler's transformation. The flip side of Lon Chaney turning into the Wolfman. In Tyler's case, the Wolfman was turning into Adonis. His arms grew longer, until the cuffs of his long-sleeved shirt were at his elbows. His pants fit him like Bermuda shorts. The seams of his shirt and pants and underwear burst like ripe fruit, allowing the new Adam to be born.

* * * * *

Manuel had told Leszek that if someone had progressed sufficiently on the "path," he or she would encounter the "double." Leszek had given as much credence to this pronouncement as he had to Manuel's belief in the powers of macho garlic.

But here he was facing his own double! What was it that Manuel had said to do in such a case? Frozen in the doorway, Leszek tried to remember. But memory, like the process of thought and the feelings of love and desire and pain, was no longer available to him.

* * * * *

Tyler felt his hair growing, felt each strand like a thread of light coming out of his head. He looked at his hands: they were large, with long symmetrical fingers, beautiful hands, a pianist's hands. He ripped off the shreds of his clothes. His body was firm, muscular, beautifully proportioned. The arches of his feet were architectural achievements.

He held out his arms, gazed at them, turned them over. He looked at his chest, his loins, his legs, he turned and tried to see his backside. He put his hands on his hair, on his face. With his heart beating madly, Tyler stepped slowly into the bathroom. He put his hands on the basin for ballast, bent his head, and tried to steady his shaking limbs and percussive heart.

* * * * *

"So," said Leszek's double, "here we are."

Leszek nodded involuntarily.

"What do you have to say to me?" asked the double.

If only I had paid more attention to Manuel's ramblings, thought Leszek.

"I'm waiting," said the double, who stood up and walked across the room until he was facing his twin.

"What do you want?" asked his counterpart, the part-time janitor.

"Look at what you've done to me," said the double as he gestured with his open hand at Leszek—a sweeping motion, as if to say: "Look at his mess."

"What have I done?" Leszek asked, only his lips moving, the rest of his body in stiff, military attention.

"You're killing me."

"Killing you?"

His double gently took hold of Leszek's elbow and led him to the window, where they could see Lake Michigan and the lights of the city. A huge moon, full and glowing, hung in the dark sky, as if God Himself were surveying the scene through a peep hole.

* * * * *

Tyler raised his head slowly, his eyes closed. When his head was level with where he thought the mirror would be, he held his eyes closed for a few more wild heartbeats and then he opened them. And then he saw himself. My God, he thought. I'm not handsome. I'm beautiful. I'm the most beautiful person I've ever seen.

* * * * *

"Look at all of this, and tell me what you want," said Leszek's double as they gazed out the window.

"I want nothing anymore," replied Leszek.

"And why is that?"

"I am too tired to want anything."

"And why are you so tired?"

"Because I am always working."

"And why are you always working?"

"Because . . ." Leszek had to stop and think, which was impossible. So, rather than think of an answer, he merely let the words come as they would. "Because I have to."

"Why do you have to?"

"Because I am supposed to. I am a man."

"Should a man kill himself with work?"

"I have a wife, a child, a home, responsibilities."

"That's not the reason you are killing us."

"Why then?"

"So you don't have to think."

"What is there to think about?"

"So you don't have to think about how you have betrayed me."

"I have been a good man. I have worked. I have kept my word. I have betrayed no one."

"I had a life," said the double. "I was born in this world to experience what it is to live. And you have killed that with your desire for real estate, your petty jealousies, your overwork, and lack of attention to the things that matter. Yes, Leszek, you have betrayed me."

Just then, a dark cloud passed in front of the moon, as if God had blinked. Leszek, too, blinked and kept blinking, something he had done since childhood to keep from crying. He knew his double was right.

* * * * *

Tyler stayed up all night studying himself in the mirror, as if he were a living, breathing sculpture. His heart was beating fast, so fast he thought he could see it bulging through his chest.

When morning came, Tyler had a plan. Go to the Salvation Army, buy a suit, and go out and get a good job. Who wouldn't hire me now, he thought.

But he couldn't leave the house. None of his old clothes fit. He'd been a runt. Now he was a titan, six and a half feet of pure muscle. He found an old oversized T-shirt, but it only came to his navel. Finally, he cut a hole in a sheet, placed the hole over his head, and wore it like a toga. He used an old necktie for a sash.

Tyler stepped out into the bright morning. In his bare feet, he walked briskly in the direction of the Salvation Army.

As he passed people in the street, they looked at him, stopped dead in their tracks, then fell to the ground, writhing in agony.

What is happening, Tyler wondered.

* * * * *

"Is it too late?" Leszek asked, his throat thick with the strain of not weeping.

"It depends," replied the double.

"Depends?"

"On how quickly you can set things right. And you must begin with Tyler."

CHAPTER 8

Brief Transit Where the Dreams Cross

For months now, Father Jeremiah Flynn had dedicated himself to fasting, praying, reading the scriptures, and meditating on the sacraments. All of these activities had one objective: a miracle.

Yes, a miracle would take place in the church. A miracle so profound that it would capture the imagination of people around the world. Sacred Heart would become the site of pilgrimages, it would host international conferences, be the subject of documentaries, receive extensive media coverage. A miracle would take place and Sacred Heart would be saved.

* * * * *

Norma Villalobos held the first meeting of "Saints and Saviors of the World" in the same VFW hall where she'd had her fateful meeting with Sister Merlina Talbott. The rental on the hall and the printing of the posters and flyers had set her back a week's salary. But now that Julio had a good-paying job as a fireman, the financial pressure was off Norma. She could use her money as she pleased. All the prayers and novenas she'd recited, all the candles she'd lit for Julio had finally paid off. But her preoccupation with "Saints and Saviors" made her take only passing notice of the boy's change in heart.

For his part, Julio was disappointed at his mother's lack of enthusiasm. He did his best to capture her attention, parading the length of the apartment in his rubber coat, boots, and fireman's hat. But Norma just looked at him as if he were a window with a view of a brick wall. More and more, Julio looked to his fellow firemen for empathy and moral support. And, long overdue, he got his own apartment.

Norma was careful not to let Julio know of her mission. She was a grown woman, yet, more than anything, she feared her son's derision. In many ways, it was as if they had changed places. All those years she, Norma, had been the respectable citizen and he, Julio, had been a member of the underworld. Now Julio was an upright, honest workingman in a respected occupation, and Norma was about to become the leader of a cult.

* * * * *

A miracle. A miracle. A miracle. This is what Jeremiah pondered as he stared trance-like into the flames of the video fireplace that played on his television screen.

The globe was spinning, time was marching inexorably toward the shortest day of the year. Each beat of Jeremiah's heart was another tick of the clock. If the parish didn't come up with a million dollars by New Year's Eve, it was curtains for his beautiful church.

Despite the fasting, praying, meditating, and keeping silent, nothing happened. Father Flynn was merely tired, hungry, and subject to a constant headache in the center of his forehead.

He gave up. Took off his glasses, turned off the fireplace, called down for supper, and turned on the news. So be it.

After his meal, Jeremiah crossed the courtyard, unlocked the side door of the church, and entered the evening silence of his temple. He crossed himself with holy water, lit a candle before the statue of Christ with his hand raised and his heart aflame, genuflected, then knelt in silent prayer. His entreaties had ceased, his mind no longer whirled, his stomach no longer growled. He was simply present.

Then he heard a voice above him. "Father, hear my confession."

* * * * *

Of course, she'd changed her name. She couldn't risk having Julio see the posters. Surely, most of these fringe religious types have stage names. Merlina couldn't have been a given name. No, Norma had to assume a separate identity for her "Saints and Saviors" work. She had decided to call herself Sister Angelina Guardina.

At the first meeting, only a trickle of woebegone types came to witness Sister Angelina's demonstration. Dressed in a white choir robe, Sister Angelina used her yard-long, rubber-tipped pointer to indicate how God's word could be gleaned from the transportation posters—the ones she had been surreptitiously gathering for weeks—which were now set up on easels around the front of the hall.

Whap, whap, whap. Her pointer beat the cardboard posters. Letter by letter, Norma demonstrated her skill. She allowed the audience to call out Bible quotations. Without missing a beat, she selected an advertisement and immediately began to spell out the quote. The effect was magical. The audience oohed and aahed at the completion of each Biblical phrase.

Norma was a matter-of-fact woman, and her presentation, despite its inherent drama, lacked the style of a seasoned performer like Sister Merlina Talbott. Norma quickly realized that she would have to do something to liven up the proceedings.

* * * * *

Jeremiah looked up, then covered his face. A shock passed through his body. He trembled. His heart palpitated.

"Please, Father," repeated the man.

Jeremiah continued to cover his face. He shook his head.

"Father, please. I beg you. Help me!" The man fell to the floor, sobbing.

Now that the man's face was out of view, Jeremiah ventured a look at his writhing form. He was dressed in a sheet. Before Jeremiah could avert his gaze, the man flipped over and looked straight into the priest's face. Quickly, Jeremiah put his head between his knees and covered it with his hands. He rocked back and forth like a frightened child.

"What can I do?" asked the man, not to the priest, but to someone higher. He laid on his back and shouted his words up to the vaulted ceiling painted with Jesus pointing to his bleeding, thorny, Sacred Heart.

"Who are you?" asked the priest, his words muffled through his black wool pants.

"I am Tyler."

* * * * *

First, Norma decided to add music. She appropriated Julio's abandoned boom box and bought several tapes of religious music, to which her growing flock ineptly sung along. She photocopied the words to simple hymns like "The Old Rugged Cross" and "How Great Thou Art," but the congregation still couldn't manage to sing either in key or on the beat.

Norma knew she needed something to lead into the actual demonstration. Sister Talbott had the Angel Uriel and his multi-colored lights. Norma needed a similarly dramatic hook. She'd heard that there were religious groups that handled snakes to prove God's protection from evil. This, indeed, was dramatic, but highly impractical. Snakes were expensive and you had to feed them live mice. Norma needed something simple, but stunning.

While casting about for an idea, Norma decided to do the next best thing. She'd use the time between the singing and the demonstration to allow people to get up and testify about the power of this particular method of serving God.

* * * * *

"Tyler?"

"Tyler Sikes."

"Tyler Sikes?"

"Yes, Tyler Sikes. I converted when I married Deeanna. I come to church every Sunday with my two children. I work at the mini-mart. You're trying to turn my divorce into an annulment . . . ."

"Tyler Sikes? But Tyler Sikes is . . . " the priest trailed off.

"Tyler Sikes was ugly. Tyler Sikes wanted to be beautiful. And now I am—but no one can look at me!"

"But, Tyler, this is a miracle."

* * * * *

"I spelled out *Cast your bread upon the waters and it will return in many days* on a Wonder Bread sign. I picked that verse cause I didn't have nothin to eat for three days. After I spelled it out, I prayed that the Lord would find me somethin to eat. I was walkin down an alley and I seen a lady throwin bread out to the birds. I walked in her yard and held out my hands, and, praise the Lord, she threw the whole loaf at me and run back in the house. It wasn't Wonder Bread, but who am I to split hairs?"

"Hallelujah!"

"Me, I picked out *He restoreth my soul, He leadeth me in the path of righteousness for His namesake* on an ad for a cocaine hotline. Praise Jesus, I haven't had a yen for crack for a week now. The Lord has healed me. I stopped stealing. The Salvation Army's helping me look for a job. I told them about you, Sister Angelina. How it was you that showed me the way!"

"Amen!"

It appeared that all the repeat visitors had a tale to tell. Norma had never counted on this. She saw her method of puzzling out the Word of God as spiritual combat—a way to push back the forces of darkness. It had never occurred to her that people's lives might be changed. That they might experience, as Sister Talbott's poster had foretold, MIRACLES! MIRACLES! MIRACLES!

* * * * *

"It's a curse. When I was ugly, people would at least look at me."

"Perhaps God has turned you into an angel," comforted the priest.

This had never occurred to Tyler. He had not wanted to be an angel. He wanted to be a man, a beautiful man. An Adonis. A new Adam.

"Pray for me," the angel-man finally said. "Pray for God to remove this curse. Tell Him I'm sorry. I'm sorry for wanting something I should never have wanted."

* * * * *

The meetings were held on Saturday evenings. For several weeks, Norma had noticed a distinguished-looking gentleman taking notes in the back row. He was especially interested in the testimonials of the flock, and couldn't seem to write fast enough when people were speaking. At first, Norma thought the man was merely taking down the lucky Biblical quotations, with a mind to trying them himself. But, no, he was writing down everything the people were saying. Norma had never seen anyone write so fast.

Because he wrote all his books in longhand, Henry was adept with a pen. He never suffered from writer's cramp. He carried three new Flair pens and a new thick notebook everywhere he went.

After seeing Sister Angelina's poster on the lamp post outside WHVN, he'd had a hunch that he could gather some useful information for his book. Henry hadn't been wrong. Here was something new, something original. Something that really developed his theme of the splintering of religion at the end of the twentieth century.

Henry didn't want to call attention to himself—he was, in fact, the only one taking notes—but he felt it would be dishonest to tape-record the proceedings. No, he would do what he was doing right out in the open. And if Sister Angelina asked what he was up to, he'd just have to tell her. After all, these religious types love publicity, don't they?

* * * * *

"Please, Father, have God change me back to the way I was."

Jeremiah's full stomach, his hour of relaxation in front of the television, his recent admission of defeat in his effort to concoct a miracle—all of these things put him in a strangely detached state. He no longer cared. He no longer wanted anything. And, in this emptiness, in this vacancy, he heard a voice. It said: "Here is your trump card. Play it."

"Tyler," Father Flynn said, "God may have something else in mind for you."

CHAPTER 9

Signs and Wonders

Leszek's encounter with his double had had a profound effect. He'd quit his janitor's job, hung up his guitar, and bid farewell to the Dixie Dandies. This left him with his 7-3:30 shift as an HVAC technician and his apprenticeship with Manuel.

Leszek was able to sleep again. He was getting back to his former weight. His thoughts were becoming more coherent. He had reestablished a harmonious relationship with his wife, who believed these changes in Leszek were the result of her frequent and fervent prayers.

Danuta even admitted to Leszek her proficiency in English. Leszek encouraged her to return to school and obtain her nursing certification. A miracle, Danuta thought.

Leszek's jealousy, the central fact of his existence, had blown over like last year's hurricane. This, like many other things—his lust for real estate, his workaholism—no longer held him in sway. He was a free man. Except for two things: his apprenticeship with Manuel and the curse on Tyler.

* * * * *

Jeremiah's plan was simple. He would invite the Cardinal for Christmas Mass. He would invite the media, citing the historic significance of the church's final Yuletide celebration. During the homily, Jeremiah would close his eyes and say, "Heavenly Father, if for any reason you do not wish Sacred Heart to close its doors, give us a sign." And then he would play his trump card.

At the proper moment, Tyler would appear in all his beauteous glory, say he was an Archangel sent by God to tell one and all that the beloved church should remain open. Then the man/angel would walk down the center aisle and out the door, leaving everyone in his stunned wake. And it would all be captured on video!

* * * * *

Leszek could not turn in his resignation to Manuel the way he had to the building managers. He could not simply reverse the curse on Tyler the way he'd changed his jealousy. These things required more than an act of will. They required a well-thought-out plan, inspiration, and, not least of all, luck. Leszek spent every waking moment trying to come up with an idea, but, try as he might, he came up empty.

Jarvis, who had become a fixture in the household, noticed that Leszek seemed preoccupied. But since Jarvis was walking on the eggs of his newly-found domestic harmony, he was reluctant to ask a direct question.

"Les, I've been very unsettled lately. But I can't quite put my finger on it."

Leszek, who was smarter than Jarvis gave him credit for, did not take the bait. "I'm sorry to hear that," he said.

"It's just that life is so demanding, so hectic these days . . . ."

"It is a busy life, yes," said Leszek.

"You think so?"

"Yes."

"How's work?"

"Fine."

"Everything all right?"

"Fine."

"Good. Just checking."

"Thank you."

"You're welcome."

Clearly, the indirect approach was getting Jarvis nowhere. He'd have to try another tactic. Being a man of extremes, he quickly moved to the opposite pole.

"You've been acting worried lately, Les. Why don't you tell me what's on your mind?"

This sudden shift caught Leszek off guard. Sure, he'd been worried lately. Worried, not to mention agitated, perplexed, and frightened. Jarvis's nudge was all he needed to bring it squirming to the surface.

"I have placed a curse on a man. And now I must find a way to take it back."

"What did the man do?"

"That is not important, what he did. What is important is what I did. His life is ruined and I must fix it."

"Have you prayed?"

"Prayed?"

"Yes."

Prayer. It was so simple that, like the thing hidden on the mantelpiece, it was the last place he'd looked.

"Kneel down and pray with me now," said Jarvis.

"Now?"

"Why wait?"

Why, indeed?

But Leszek no longer felt worthy of prayer. It was a lost language. He shook his head and left the room.

I shouldn't have come on so strong, thought Jarvis. Now the poor man will probably never pray again.

* * * * *

"What if later they recognize me on the street? What then?" asked Tyler.

"Fold your hands, bow your head, and act like a visitation. Then vamoose. They'll think they're being haunted."

"So, if I do this, will you help me?"

"I said I would."

"How?"

"My friend, Dr. Cummings, plastic surgeon to the stars, will have a look at you. I'm sure he can do something."

"You mean, I'd have to be operated on?" Tyler had a deep fear of anesthesia-induced comas. It had happened to Senator Buckmeister right when he was ready to blow the lid off a CIA scheme in *The Madrid Plot*.

"How else?"

"I thought, you know, maybe *you* could do something."

"I'm a priest, not a magician, Tyler."

"There's a difference?"

* * * * *

Leszek closed the bathroom door and turned on the water in the basin. He was on the verge of weeping and wanted to cover the sound.

He faced himself in the mirror, looking dead in his own eyes. Steam rose from the basin, where the hot water ran—an extravagant action that, in the old days, would have sent Leszek's spartan soul into spasms. Beads of sweat formed on his brow, dripped from his nose, covered his cheeks. Steam curled around his face, through his hair. This is what I will look like in hell, Leszek thought.

Leszek clasped the basin and stiffened his arms. He had a mental image of playing medicine ball, but his arms stayed at his sides and the ball went right through him, leaving a huge hole in the center of his chest. In the mirror, Leszek could see all the way through the hole in his body to the shelf of shampoo and Kleenex on the opposite wall. He imagined going through life this way. A man with a hole in his center, a man with no soul.

As Leszek watched the steam swathe his head and face, as he looked through the hole in his center, he knew with absolute certainty that he was doomed. He began to cry, but his face was already so wet with sweat and steam that his tears left no mark, merely blended into the mass of water that Leszek was slowly becoming.

Suddenly aware of his surroundings, suddenly registering the running water, Leszek now had another urge, which made him cry still harder. His body was continually making demands—feed me, give me drink, relieve me. And now, when he was so deep in thought, when he was getting this glimpse into his state of grace, why now did his body have to make a demand?

The body and its water: its tears, its sweat, spit, its full bladder. Leszek felt like a human water balloon, with just the thinnest layer of skin holding it all in. One sudden move, one brush up against a nail, and pop—his whole life would go pouring down some rusty drain.

Leszek had a deep urge to take a shower. He wanted to stand under the water, let it flow over his head, his body, his front, his back, his face. He wanted to open his mouth and let the hot water pour in.

A knock at the door.

"You okay in there?" Jarvis asked.

Leszek flushed the toilet, hoping the old man would take a hint from the noise.

It's hard to get any peace around here, Leszek thought. It's hard to get any peace anywhere. It's hard to get any peace, period.

Something new entered Leszek's awareness. Plop, plop, plop. The faucet in the bathtub. Why hadn't he replaced the washer? He was becoming so lazy. He was letting everything go. As soon as the dripping entered his consciousness, with its monotonous rhythm, its steady beat, there was no way to tune it out.

Rather than try to block out the sound, rather than try to resist the drip, drip, dripping noise, Leszek, perhaps for the first time in his life, really listened to it. He measured the silences between the drips. He closed his eyes and mentally saw the drain where the water collected, saw the water swirling down the hole, through the pipes, under the ground, down to the deep places in the earth, where the element seeks its level.

In his mind, the drain became larger and larger, a spinning star of water. Listening to the steady drip, drip, drip, contemplating the spinning drain, Leszek was experiencing something for the first time in years. His mind, his moving, jumping, leaping, jabbering mind, was completely still. And, in the stillness, he felt a soothing peace descend.

And then he knew how he would remove the curse from Tyler.

* * * * *

Jeremiah gave a heavy sigh. It always came down to this. Simple people, simple minds. The whole lot of them thought he had magical powers.

"My good man, I am not a conjurer."

Tyler, who had once read a book called *The Conjurer's Conundrum*, got the point. The priest was, after all, only a man. A man who had studied holy books—but a man nonetheless. All Tyler could hope was that, like a learned attorney, the priest's studies had made him aware of some loophole in God's laws. Maybe the priest knew of a precedent for reversing an answered prayer.

"So, are we agreed?" the priest asked.

Tyler believed he was, and had always been, an unlucky man. And, if this plan followed true-to-form, it would prove a disaster.

"Agreed," Tyler finally said.

CHAPTER 10

The Angelus

Norma missed Catholicism. Missed the comforting structure of the Mass. Missed the prayers, the rituals, the trappings. She'd already forgotten how disenchanted she had become with her religion such a short time ago. She longed for it now.

Catholicism was a religion of wanting, a religion of works. It was a religion whereby God said: "So, what have you done for me lately?" It was a religion of uncertainty, where the slightest errant footfall would send you sliding into eternal perdition.

Norma missed the suspense and insecurity of the Catholic faith. To be honest, the Evangelical sects were, well, boring. You accepted Jesus and that was it. You told the same dull story over and over of how you were saved.

Catholicism was so tied to Norma's cultural life, that its loss had left her feeling like someone without a heritage, without a history, without an identity.

She wanted her former life back, but she couldn't just abandon her flock. They'd already raised the money and were drawing up plans for a permanent dwelling.

Norma rarely prayed anymore. She was too embarrassed, feeling that she had no right to address the Almighty. Yet, on this particular occasion, as she sat in her red Lincoln Town Car pondering the waves of Lake Michigan, Norma bowed her head and bit the bullet. She prayed, promised, prostrated her soul. She pulled out all the stops and begged God to help her.

* * * * *

Tyler's days were measured by the tolling of the Angelus at morning, noon, and evening. The altar boys had been relieved of this particular duty. Father Flynn could not afford to have Tyler discovered. So, Tyler was now the ringer of the bells.

Like Quasimodo, Tyler was holed up in a bell tower. Unlike Quasimodo, who had taken refuge in the belfry because of his ugliness, Tyler hid there to escape the curse of his beauty.

Father Flynn installed a portable space heater, an old wind-up Big Ben clock, blankets, a Coleman lantern, and a variety of theological works. Reading Teilhard de Chardin was not the same as reading Nigel Clive. Tyler was cold, he was bored, he was restless. And the bell ringing was giving him migraines. He hoped this would all be over soon. He marked off each day with a giant red "X" on the wall of the bell tower.

To relieve his restlessness, to bring some blood back into his cold bones, once a day he ventured down to the church. During the day, the church was locked against burglars. And when Tyler heard Sister Ludmilla turn the key, he crept down the winding stairs.

Like a prisoner in his cell, Tyler had measured the distance of the church's aisles to arrive at a mile. From front to back, to the center aisle, genuflect, down the center aisle to the altar, genuflect, to the next corner, to the back, to the center, genuflect, and on and on he paced out a seven-minute mile. His lithe, classical legs took him around the church quickly, until all he saw was a blur of colored glass and candles. After an hour, he climbed the winding stairs and fell into an exhausted sleep, disturbed by dreams of oversleeping and forgetting to ring the evening bells.

Today, Tyler had just finished his second mile when he discovered that he wasn't alone.

* * * * *

Norma prayed, but felt nothing. No tingles up and down her spine, no prickles in her scalp, no tears, no butterflies in her stomach. She forged on, her feeble faith pulling her along like her Grandma's worn-out mule. Eke it out step by step, Norma. Put one word in front of the other. *Hail* and then *Mary* and then *full* and then *of* and then *grace*, and then keep trying, say the words whether you feel anything or not.

She opened her eyes and rested her head on the back of the seat. She watched as a slate-gray wave broke through the ice floes of the lake and rose up above the water. The wave climbed higher and higher, and still Norma thought of nothing. Did not even register the strangeness of it. She just watched, until a wall of water inched forward like a snail. The wave heaved itself up on the shore and moved forward until it stood right in front of the sleek hood of Norma's car. Then the wave lit up like a movie screen.

* * * * *

When Tyler saw Henry Purcell duck out of the confessional, he had the simultaneous urge to embrace him and to flee. Instead, he hid behind the statue of Saint Michael and watched as Henry crept around the church.

Henry, well into his book now, was working on a chapter about the demise of the inner-city temples of Catholicism. He wanted to get the details right, so he hid in the confessional until the door was locked. He needed a few hours by himself to peruse the interior of Sacred Heart.

Henry thought he was alone, until he heard Tyler scream. When he turned, he saw someone on fire at the back of the church. The man fell to the ground, trying to stifle the flames.

Tyler had been so intent on watching Henry that he'd backed up into a row of candles. Now he was on fire and couldn't get away. He was about to face another person who would see him and fall down in pain. He looked up. Henry was right there, staring him straight in the face.

Henry was a handsome old man. He was also vain about his looks. Even when he was alone, he was reluctant to put on his glasses and destroy the spell. So, when he encountered Tyler, he thought, "Nice-looking chap," and nothing more. His vision was blurred just enough to take the edge off of Tyler's preternatural beauty.

"Do you want some water?" Henry asked.

"I'm not thirsty," Tyler said, and wondered why the man could look at him without keeling over.

"I meant for the fire. Is it out?"

"It's out," Tyler said as he stood up.

"You work here?" Henry asked.

"Off and on," Tyler said, and turned to face the wall.

"I was wondering if you could show me where the priests change their clothes."

"It's locked."

"How about the bell tower?"

"Locked, too."

"What do you do around here?"

"I fill in."

"How do you feel about the church closing?"

"If it's God's will . . . ."

"Who's to say what is and what is not God's will?"

"God."

"And how do we hear what He has to say?"

"When the time comes, He'll let us know."

"Would you mind sitting down and answering a few questions?"

"About what?"

"I'm working on a book about religion. Henry Purcell."

Henry extended his hand. But, since Tyler was still turned to the wall, he didn't see the gesture. And since Henry's vision was operating at half speed, he momentarily lost sight of Tyler, thinking his inert form was another of the church's many statues.

"Still there?" Henry asked.

"Henry Purcell from the radio?"

"The same."

"You mean, you're blind?"

* * * * *

From her car, Norma watched as images appeared in the wave of water. First, she saw a tree, then a river, then a man, then a woman. The images drew themselves on the screen, like an Etch-a-Sketch. Norma watched as one line, then another, then another formed on the screen, looking like nothing, just a group of lines — until suddenly a pattern emerged and a shape was there: a tree, a river, a man, a woman.

The man and the woman stood beneath the tree, then jumped into the river and flowed from one edge of the screen to the other, back and forth, back and forth. Then the river washed them up on shore and they stood under the tree. A cloud drew itself above them and it started to rain — tiny black lines on the screen.

The man and the woman lifted their hands, inviting the rain to wash over them. Then the tiny lines of rain stopped, the cloud faded away, and a circle with tiny black lines around it drew itself slowly in the sky. Quickly, flowers appeared on the ground. Then, a house, drawn as a child would draw one.

A man, a woman, a tree, a river, a cloud, a sun, flowers, and a house. Civilization.

Suddenly, the wave lurched forward and covered Norma's car. The water seeped in—through the windshield, the back window, the doors—filling up the car inch by inch. Norma sat and let the water rise up over her. A fishbowl, she thought. Yes, here I sit, a fish in a bowl. She didn't fight it, just let it happen. She gripped the steering wheel and felt the cold, cold water rise up over her.

* * * * *

"Blind? No, no. Why would you think that?" Henry said.

"You don't seem to be seeing me."

"Well, all right, if it's like that, I'll put on my glasses."

"No!"

"No?"

"Leave them off."

"Why is that?"

"If you want me to talk to you, I don't want you to see me the way I am."

"And what way is that?"

"I'm cursed. That's why I live here."

At this news, Henry's journalistic juices started to flow. Sounded like something from the Middle Ages. Sanctuary in a church. Just the thing for the book. What a metaphor. And he had just stumbled upon it.

"All right. If you'll tell me all about it, I'll leave my glasses off. Mind if I tape you?"

Tyler had a mental image of being bound with duct tape. Occupational hazard—too many hold-ups at the mini-mart.

Henry took out a tape recorder from his jacket pocket.

"Only if you promise not to use my name."

"What is your name?"

"Just call me Cain. Like him, I'm marked, cast out."

"All right, Cain. Start at the beginning and tell me how you came to set up camp in this doomed, domed cathedral."

Henry led Tyler to the church's front pew. They sat in the shadow of the giant crucifix.

"Just begin anywhere you want."

"Well, see, I was born an ugly kid, but I always wanted to be beautiful . . . ."

Henry sighed. An old story. The oldest. He only hoped there'd be some original spin on the theme. He needed something powerful for the home stretch. The book was due at the publisher's in a week.

Lucky for Henry, Tyler was not about to let him down.

CHAPTER 11

Water Music

After trying in vain to rescue Norma from her car, a jogger called the fire department.

When Julio arrived on the scene, he didn't recognize his mother. The floating body reminded Julio of Esther Williams, whose many movies he had watched at three or four in the morning when he'd returned keyed-up from his jaunts with the Latin Lords. Many times, Julio had fallen asleep fully dressed, while watching the swimmer glide through the water. Then he dreamed of an underwater world where Esther Williams was the very spirit of the sea, a mythological creature who provided order to the submerged landscape.

As the firefighters prepared to rescue the woman, Julio looked through the window on the driver's side. The black hair stood out straight, the eyes bulged, tiny bubbles escaped from the nose and mouth. A firefighter pulled on each door, but the doors wouldn't budge. They took levers and tried to pry open the doors, but no luck. Meanwhile, the woman was drowning in her car.

Julio had no idea that his mother owned a red Lincoln Town Car. Norma had managed to keep her double life a secret from her son. After phoning his mother at her job and learning she no longer worked there, Julio questioned Norma, who informed him she had taken a job at a firm that did not allow personal phone calls.

Norma still lived in the same apartment and, when Julio came to visit, still wore her familiar clothes. She had purchased no new furniture nor appliances. All of the new trappings of her life were relegated to the Lake Shore Drive apartment she had rented in the name Angelina Guardina.

A firefighter handed Julio an ax and told him to break the rear window. Another firefighter was busy at the windshield. Others worked on the locks with acetylene torches.

Firefighter O'Malley lifted an ax and hit the windshield with all his strength. A dead-on hit. The window popped out and air rushed into the vacuum — sending Norma flying and clearing her lungs of water. She shot through the air and was propelled into the icy lake. Norma's thick ranch mink coat, though wet, broke her fall as she landed on a large mass of ice. She sat up, dazed, as the ice floated farther away from shore.

A wind blew up, a cold high wind that made a path in the icy lake. All Norma saw was a blur of lights as the wind swept her block of ice to the center of the lake.

"Call the Coast Guard, O'Malley," one of the firefighters said.

As water sloshed from the car, Julio reached into the glove compartment, looking for the registration. He found a mass of soggy flyers advertising the skills of Sister Angelina, healer and prophet.

"Come on, Villalobos. The cops are here. Let them handle it."

Julio handed the contents of the glove compartment to one of Chicago's finest. Then he turned and looked at the lake. The lady was just a tiny dot now, moving farther and farther from shore.

When the news broke that Sister Angelina was drifting out on the lake, a group of her followers amassed for a candlelight vigil.

And Henry Purcell, news bloodhound that he was, smelled another good story. He took the night off, telling the station to repeat a program he'd done on Native American poets.

When he arrived on the scene, Henry laid back for a moment before joining the crowd. This was one of his favorite parts—watching things unfold, taking the lay of the land, figuring out the dynamics of the event.

Sister Angelina Guardina had been one of Henry's favorite subjects. He'd liked her so much that he'd felt like asking her out to dinner. But it wouldn't be ethical to fraternize with the subject matter. Still, Sister Angelina was really something.

Sister Angelina's explanation of her gift could have been lifted from the pages of a treatise on quantum mechanics—the observer changes the experiment. That's why she was able to find any Bible verse in any ad on any branch of public transportation. Sister Angelina, for all her religion, was one of the most pragmatic people Henry had ever met.

It had made an interesting chapter in *Mixed Messages*. God, how he loved his book. He loved all of his books, but never more than when he was in the thick of them. The theme taking shape, patterns emerging, new avenues opening up, ideas popping—Henry loved the book the way a proud father loves his darling child.

And now *this*—more excitement, more drama, another chapter to add to the pile. Though Henry felt deeply for Sister Angelina's plight, his writerly self was ecstatic. What a story!

Henry sauntered up to the assembly of Angelinites, police, Coast Guard, and media types and, like a rat slipping through a tight hole in a wall, blended unnoticed into the crowd.

Henry eased up to a weeping woman with two small children in tow. "What happened?" Henry asked innocently. This was always his approach in these situations. Act as if he knew nothing.

"Sister Angelina was too good for this world," the woman said through her tears.

"Why is that?"

"She found a way to change the world, so Satan snatched her away."

"Satan?"

"The devil."

"How could the devil have power over one of God's anointed?"

"Even Jesus fell prey to the devil. God gives the great liar free rein over this earthly coil."

"But what happened? How did Sister Angelina wind up in the middle of the lake?"

"Satan snatched her away."

Henry realized he was going to get no more than an editorial view from this sobbing devotee. He wanted facts: when, where, why, how, what. He walked over to the perimeter of the police encampment, hoping to pick up a clue.

"Just shot out like a cannon," Henry heard one of them say.

"God only knows how her car got filled up with water."

"And *her* a preacher. What does that say for the rest of us?"

"Yeah, there's no hope for me, that's a fact."

The police officers laughed the warm, conspiratorial laugh of three men out on a cold night's assignment. They lifted the plastic lids on their styrofoam cups of coffee. Steam rose into the night, making ghostly shapes before it faded in the frigid air.

* * * * *

Norma, whose wet clothes and body had frozen into a statue-like form, was completely immobile, except for her eyes. This is what it's like to be buried alive, she thought. Alive burial was one of Norma's deepest fears. It had happened to several people in her native village. One man, after being buried alive three times, had even invented a life-detection monitor to be used upon subsequent burials.

The shore lights dimmed as she drifted out farther and farther, and Norma felt herself pulled deeper and deeper into total darkness. Then my eyes, too, will be useless, she thought. In this she was wrong.

As soon as Norma was totally engulfed in blackness, she began to see darting streams of light. Then a circle of transparent beings surrounded her.

"Why did you jump?" one of them asked.

Norma, whose mouth was frozen shut, said nothing, hoping it was only an hallucination, a symptom of the great shock she'd suffered.

"She didn't jump because she was poor like me. Look at that coat. A mink, yet," said another being.

"Probably caught her husband cheating."

"Maybe she has cancer."

"Or depression, like me."

"Maybe her kids drove her crazy."

"Maybe she was on her way to prison, like me."

"Maybe she embezzled funds from her company."

"Or she's in love with her priest."

"She was probably drunk and just fell in."

The transparent beings continued to speculate as to why Norma had jumped in the lake. After all, why else would she be there? More and more beings appeared, hundreds of them, all lost souls who had taken a final plunge to end their many and assorted troubles.

"Is she dead yet?" one of them asked.

"Not quite."

"Soon, though."

With this, a gleeful tittering arose. Soon, she would join them. Soon, Norma Villalobos would be another lost spirit of the lake.

A foghorn broke through the levity.

"Nuts!" one of them said.

"Let's hope they don't find her."

"Let's hope she dies soon."

"Then we'll know why she jumped."

They all said in unison: "Why she jumped! Why she jumped! Why she jumped!"

Norma managed to pry her frozen lips free.

"I didn't jump, you fools. I was thrown."

The beings gasped. "Thrown?"

"Yes," she snarled at them.

"Who threw you?"

"God."

With that, the beings faded away, and Norma was left alone amid the ice and the blackness.

It wasn't the shock, the fear, the pain, or the loneliness that bothered her. It was the forced inactivity. The very thing that had gotten her into so much trouble in the first place. She had started picking out Bible verses on public transportation because she did not want to waste time. Even now, Norma had to fight the urge to recite all the movies she'd ever seen, or to try to picture her girlhood bedroom.

One thing she *did* know. Prayer was out.

CHAPTER 12
Light My Fire

Danuta was working the night shift at the hospital. Leszek was performing his daily payback to Manuel. Jarvis, who had moved into the spare bedroom, was making poetry notes in the kitchen, while listening for Sandra's steady breathing in the other room. The old judge could not have been happier. A lovely, kind, surrogate daughter; a beautiful, charming granddaughter—not to mention a cozy roof over his head, hearty meals, and interesting work.

Jarvis's years on the bench had left their mark. He could tune out any distraction. It wasn't until smoke filled the kitchen, obscuring his view of the yellow legal pad, that he looked up. When he turned to the window and saw the nearness of the smoke and flames, he ran to the bedroom, scooped up Sandra in her down quilt, and ran from the house, his legal pad under his arm.

But where could he go? It was late. Perhaps someone at the scene of the fire would give them refuge. But he didn't want to get that close, not with the child. Jarvis had to think of something fast—the child in his arms was growing heavier by the second, and he didn't want to drop her. He decided to go to Sacred Heart.

* * * * *

It had taken Leszek a while to track down Tyler. But, really, it was the most logical place to look. Where else could an angel go, except to church?

* * * * *

121

When Jarvis arrived, he was happy to find the church open. Leszek, who was at this moment making his way up to the bell tower, had only minutes before jimmied the lock.

Jarvis deposited the still-sleeping Sandra in the first pew. And, as if the interruption had never happened, he began to write in his legal pad. The only difference was that now, instead of the kitchen, Jarvis was sitting before the altar of God.

* * * * *

The stairs creaked and groaned as Leszek inched his way to the bell tower.

"Who's there?"

Leszek stopped and waited.

"Who is it?"

Slowly, Leszek took another step.

"What do you want?"

Leszek held his breath.

"Say something."

Leszek stopped. In the darkness of the church's high tower, this disembodied voice could have been God Himself, the voice of heaven: WHO'S THERE? WHO IS IT? WHAT DO YOU WANT?

A host of chemicals shot through Leszek's body. From inside, his body shook as if he were on a fast-moving train. It took all of his effort to try to stand still. He waited. After a few minutes, Leszek heard the body above him sigh the relieved sigh of danger averted.

Leszek waited until he heard snoring above him. Now it would be easy. It could happen quickly. He wouldn't have to creep up the stairs. He could bound upward and catch his prey unaware.

With this, Leszek's heart deflated. The chemicals in his body resumed their normal flow. The certainty of success brought with it a sense of disappointment. Now, only a sense of duty carried him forward. With ultimate weariness, Leszek began to plod up the winding stairway, feeling his jacket pocket for the can of lighter fluid and the kitchen matches.

* * * * *

The fire Jarvis had seen didn't start with a cigarette—smoking was not allowed at WHVN. It didn't start because of poor wiring. It didn't start because of greasy rags, old newspapers, or dying embers from the fireplace in the station's English study. It started when the station manager, depressed at WHVN's further fall in the ratings, set fire to the latest Arbitron rating book, and left it to burn out in the metal trash can.

Only it didn't burn out. As soon as the station manager had gone, the fire drank in air from an open window. The fire shot arrows of flames to the curtains, the mahogany desk, the carpet, the bull's-eye adorned with Mick Jagger's snarling photo.

The smoke detector went off, but no one heard it. No one was at the station, except Henry, who was holed up in the studio with his guest, Sister Angelina Guardina.

"Now, tell us about your rescue, Sister Guardina."

"Call me Norma, if you don't mind, Mr. Purcell."

"Norma?"

"My real name. My recent experiences have shown me that I must give up my double life."

"Well, Nora . . . "

"Nor*ma*."

"Nor*ma*, just open up and tell our listeners your fantastic tale of rescue in the icy waters of Lake Michigan. And, listeners, this tale is not for the faint of heart. Continue, Sister Norma."

"Well, Mr. Purcell, as I said, after I encountered the spirits of the lake, I tried to still my mind. For me, this is difficult."

"Si, yo simpatico. I have the same problem."

"Most humans do."

Henry did not like to be reminded that he was like other mortals. So he did what he always did when he was either annoyed, at a loss for words, or wanted a private moment with his guest. He pressed the button.

You are listening to WHVN-FM, the voice of heaven.

* * * * *

Leszek told himself that he'd stick around long enough to make sure the man didn't die—he didn't want that on his conscience or on his soul. He would just allow Tyler to blaze until his beauty was burned away and the curse lifted.

In a distant part of himself, Leszek knew that he should turn back and go home. But another, now stronger, part of Leszek was saying: Doesn't God ask for burnt offerings?

At the top of the stairs, Leszek was about to light a match to see his way, but he stopped when he saw a glow coming from the other side of the platform. A light from a window? A lamp? No. The glowing was coming from Tyler himself—a radiance like the halo around a light bulb. Slowly, Leszek walked the distance to the sleeping body. When Leszek was within a foot of the man, Tyler turned over, his face now in full view.

Leszek doubled over. He felt as if he had been stabbed in the stomach. "Keep your eyes closed. Keep your eyes closed, and just do it. Do it!" he told himself.

At this moment, Tyler was dreaming he was playing trumpet in a Big Band at a swank hotel on New Year's Eve. He was dressed in a tuxedo and was performing one of his favorite tunes—"Stardust."

As Leszek removed the can of lighter fluid from his pocket, Tyler's heart started to pound wildly. "Wake up, you fool! Wake up!" Tyler turned over and groaned: "Leave me alone, I'm trying to sleep." His heart tried to rouse him with wild, palpitating beats. His head tried to keep him asleep with steady rationalizations.

Like a child playing Blind Man's Bluff, Leszek sought his mark. He listened for the man's breathing, leaning in closer and closer. When he could feel Tyler's hot breath on his face, Leszek lifted the can and started to squeeze.

"I tried to warn you," said Tyler's heart.

"Leave him alone," said Tyler's mind.

Tyler dreamed that it was raining fire—huge drops of water that burst into flames when they hit a mark. Then the flames grew wings and flew up in the sky.

Still, Tyler slept. Even an apocalyptic dream couldn't rouse him.

Leszek squirted, then struck a kitchen match. He leaned down and smelled for the lighter fluid. Then he threw the flame.

* * * * *

After the announcement, Henry scooted up in his chair, the better to see Norma. There was something about her, all right.

"So, Sister, after the spirits departed, you were alone, waiting for rescue?"

"That's right, Mr. Purcell."

"Henry's the name, talkin's the game."

"Yes, I was waiting for rescue . . . Henry." Norma wondered why her host was looking at her so intently. She wondered if he were trying to read her soul, like Uncle Nestor always used to when candy was missing.

"So what did you do? Did you pray? You, after all, are a woman of the cloth."

"No, I did not pray. As I stated earlier, it was because of my prayers that I was propelled into the lake."

"So, what then, Normita?"

"I stilled my mind, that was all. I felt that if I let my mind wander, I would die. So, I brought my mind to rest and then the rescue came."

"Tell us how."

"The Saints came. They said they were always with me, only I couldn't see them. I tried too hard. My mind got in the way of my faith."

"What did the Saints do?"

"They led me to a shiny silver disc, which was hovering above the water. A stairway came down and they held my arms and helped me climb the stairs. Then I was inside, where it was warm and cozy, like the house of everyone's grandmother."

"Are you sure you weren't hallucinating, Sister?"

"I am sure."

"How can you be so certain? Surely, you had just suffered a great shock."

"I am a level-headed woman. I have, as you say, suffered *many* shocks in my life. But I have never hallucinated. Even my dreams are ordinary."

"Are you sure you were rescued by Saints? The silver disc sounds like an extraterrestrial vehicle."

"They called themselves Saints, they had halos, they wore the clothes of Saints. Yes, I am sure they were Saints."

"What is it that makes someone a saint?" Henry asked.

Yes, thought Norma, what indeed?

* * * * *

When Tyler finally woke up, he thought he was self-destructing like the information tapes in his favorite TV show. As he looked at the flames leaping from his chest and arms, he remembered Grandma Wilson back home, who had burst into flames sitting in her rocking chair. Spontaneous combustion, he thought. The fire within is now without.

Tyler looked at his fiery body, felt the searing pain, but was somewhere else. Burning alive was simply too much for his spirit, which had fled across the room like a scared mouse. As his spirit cowered in the corner, Tyler's body was left alone to contend with the flames and the pain.

Meanwhile, Leszek stood by with a blanket, ready to extinguish the fire after ample damage had been done.

Yes, thought Leszek, the man is in flames, but the man is not being consumed. It is like watching a cheaply-made movie where you know the fire has been placed later over the film. People moving through burning buildings that are not really burning. Or like those fake fireplaces at Sears with the orange papers blowing around. I cannot wait here all night! I should have brought kerosene.

* * * * *

Norma was lost in thought. This would not work on the radio. Dead air was death. Henry repeated the question.

"Sister Norma, please tell us: What makes someone a saint?"

"The Pope."

"No, I mean the first principle, the root cause. What, essentially, is a saint? Share that with our listeners, Sister Norma Angelina Guardina."

"A saint is someone . . . " Norma trailed off.

As Norma pondered, Henry pressed the button.

You are listening to WHVN, the voice of heaven on your FM dial.

Yes, thought Norma, what is a saint? Is it someone who is born so good, they are never tempted? No. Is it someone who overcomes the flesh? Sometimes. Yet, there are Saints, like the good thief, who lead bad lives and only turn around at the end. Is it someone who always does the right thing? No. Think of Saint Augustine, think of Thomas Aquinas. What is it that makes someone a saint? There must be many saints, common people, who have never been recognized by the Church, who are unheralded, but have lived the lives of saints, nonetheless.

Norma had a sudden vision of the thousands upon thousands of saints who had walked the earth since the beginning of time. They held hands and circled the planet at the equator. They stood shoulder to shoulder from pole to pole. They filled the rivers, the oceans—their heads bobbing one right next to the other, like haloed buoys—lines and lines of them, until there was room for not one more.

"Can you answer me, Sister? I'm sure our listeners are as eager for your response as I am."

"A saint is someone . . . someone who tries."

"Tries what?"

"Just tries. Keeps trying, even if they fail. They don't lose heart. They are saints because they have hope."

"So, a saint can make mistakes?"

"Oh, yes. Even Saint Catherine, during the rescue, she helped me off with my mink coat, asked if she could try it on. And she didn't give it back."

"So saints can covet, steal?"

"I am sure that someday she will give it back. That is the beauty of being human. We have chances to undo our wrongs."

"And what about you, Sister Norma?"

"Me?"

"What are your wrongs?"

"Too many to mention."

"We have two minutes till commercial. Please begin . . . ."

"My wrongs are legion. More than legion."

"For example . . . ."

"Pride, most of all. Pride and . . . ."

Henry was never to hear the enumeration of Norma's wrongs. For, at that moment, smoke started to seep under the door. Henry, like Norma, was too pragmatic to allow even the desire for an interesting revelation to sway him from saving his own life.

"Listeners, I'll have to sign off now. This is Henry Purcell, the voice of reason in an unreasoning world, saying . . . goodnight."

Then, Henry pressed the button one last time.

You are listening to WHVN-FM, the voice of heaven.

* * * * *

As Tyler's spirit cringed in the corner, as Leszek waited with the blanket, a line of flames suddenly moved from the top of Tyler's head to the bottom of his torso. Like a zipper, the flames moved down Tyler's body, opening it up. A new being arose out of the burning shell, which consumed itself in flames—shriveling up like a piece of old, brittle newspaper.

The new being—a being even more beautiful than the previous one—walked toward Leszek, who was paralyzed in place like Lot's wife. The new Tyler yanked the blanket free from Leszek's stiff hands and, with perfect élan, swirled it like a kingly cape over his shoulders. Then, Tyler walked to the corner to collect his spirit.

* * * * *

The room filled with smoke. The walls bulged. The flames roared outside the door. The heat rose. Henry kissed Norma.

It was in the midst of this kiss that Julio and his fellow firefighters burst in to rescue the pair.

Little did Henry know that Julio was none other than Gabriel, the pseudonymous gang leader whom he had interviewed and, it had turned out, supplied with such useful advice about leaving the gang. And, certainly, little did Henry know that Julio was none other than dear Norma's son.

The last thing Henry remembered before he passed out was saying, "God bless you, son."

Norma, whose adrenaline was working overtime, lapsed into the pride mode and started to tell Julio and his fellow firefighters what to do. But she, too, passed out before she got very far.

So, thought Julio as he started to drag his mother out of the building, Mama's got something going with Enrique. And, despite the direness of the situation, Julio smiled. What a pair, he thought. They both know everything, they're both always right, they've both got it all figured out. Yes, thought Julio, they deserve each other.

* * * * *

Tyler looked at the paralyzed Leszek and asked his spirit: "Who's he?"

Tyler's spirit replied: "The Polack who beat himself up. He probably came here for revenge. Only how did he know it was us?"

"Yeah, how did he know? And there's something else."

"What?"

"I smell smoke."

CHAPTER 13
Mea Culpa

Driving home, Danuta saw smoke and flames in all directions. As she got nearer and nearer to home and closer and closer to the fire, she hoped and prayed that the fire was not coming from her own house.

Danuta's mind leaped to the worst possible conclusions. The house burnt to the ground, her child asphyxiated, Mr. Jarvis burnt like a piece of bacon, her husband dead trying to save the other two. To add to this already bleak scene, Danuta saw herself arrested and convicted of triple murder. It had to be her fault. She was sure she had left the iron plugged into the basement wall, where no one would notice it.

Ironing her uniform, she had been preoccupied, thinking of the thousand tasks that the day held for her. Yes, I am sure I left the iron plugged in, she thought. It is all my fault. I have burnt my house, killed my family, probably everyone on the block. Yes, they will put me in jail before I even have a chance to make amends—before I have the chance to take my own life. I will spend years in jail, live to an advanced age, then I will die and I will go to hell.

Because of the fire trucks, the crowds, the hoses, the flames, and the smoke, Danuta had to park a few blocks away and walk the rest of the way home. As she walked, she embroidered the black pictures in her mind.

In jail, the ghosts of my child, Mr. Jarvis, and my husband will appear. The child will be crying, Mr. Jarvis will say "guilty" over and over, my husband will be holding the Sunbeam iron above his head like the Statue of Liberty's torch. I will be unable to escape from these visitations. I will go crazy. I will try to starve myself dead, like that man in Ireland. But they will not let me. I will be strapped down to a table and fed through tubes in my nose.

Danuta started running, and the pictures in her mind raced, as well. Strapped to the table, the tubes running through my nose, the prison guards—each with a hot Sunbeam iron set on "steam"—will come at me and start to iron my body. My body will be covered in triangle-shaped burns, which will swell up, until I look like a clown in pantaloons.

They will take me from the table and make me perform in front of all the other prisoners—the act where the clown must sweep away the spotlight. Forever and ever I will be trying to sweep away that spotlight, to the vulgar laughter of murderers, bank robbers, and worse offenders. When I get weak, they will again strap me to the table and feed me through tubes. Then they will make me perform the spotlight act once again. Over and over, until I die and go to hell.

When Danuta was halfway down the block and saw that her house was not burning, she stopped. She looked at her chest and could see her heart pounding. She was breathing so hard, she was certain that she was depleting all of the remaining oxygen in the neighborhood. She looked. The fire was coming not from her house, but from behind her house.

Danuta ran the final steps to her home, ran around the back, and from her yard viewed the fire at WHVN-FM, the voice of heaven. Her first impulse was relief, not only that her family had been spared, but also because the music from the station would cease to play on the metal objects in her home.

She took out her keys and entered through the back door. She called for Jarvis, she called for Leszek, she ran into Sandra's room and saw her daughter's empty bed. Then she saw Jarvis's note on the kitchen table.

Dearest Barbara,
  There is a fire across the alley. Have taken Sandra to Sacred Heart. Did not know how to inform Les.
  Love,
  Jarvis

Danuta decided it would be quicker to set off for the church on foot. And, as she ran, she prayed continuously, repeating over and over: "Thank you God, thank you Jesus, thank you Blessed Virgin, thank you Angels, and thank you Saints. Thank you that my house did not burn, that my family was not harmed."

As she rounded a corner, she came face to face with what she thought was an apparition. Had her prayers been so fervent that she had conjured up this image? Was this an extension of the feverish pictures that had just played in her mind? She wanted to take another look, but lowered her eyes instead. That one glimpse had made her feel faint.

"Better turn back, there's a fire down there," the apparition said.

"No, but the fire is the other way. At WHVN."

"The fire I'm talking about is at Sacred Heart."

* * * * *

When Henry came to and heard about the fire at Sacred Heart, he tried to jump out of bed and run to the scene. He had to be restrained by two burly attendants and a humorless nurse who reminded Henry of his Aunt Edna, the taxidermist.

"Please let me up. I can't miss this. See, I'm writing a book. The fact that the church is burning is important."

"Of course it's important," clucked the nurse.

"I mean it's important to my book."

"Is that all it is to you? Material? You writers are all alike."

Henry looked at the nurse's name badge and remembered Tennessee Williams talking on the program about his nervous breakdown, and naming the horrible nurse who had attended him. I can't believe it, thought Henry. Now, when I need comfort and aid, I get the model for Sister Felicity in *Suddenly Last Summer*.

"Please," begged Henry, "I need to go."

"You're too weak."

"I feel fine."

"If you get up now, you may faint. Or have a heart episode. You need to rest. You're an old man."

Old man! Who was this bloodless, humorless, chinless nurse to call him an old man? Age, chronological years, had no meaning for Henry. He felt life surging through his body, was interested in everything around him, had unbounded curiosity. How could anyone ever consider him old? Especially now that he was in love, in love for the first time since Elaine had died seven years before.

God knows he'd been lonely during those years. He'd longed for love. But it hadn't happened. But why now? And why with this woman? After a long winter, love had come the way spring comes— it was there through no work of his own, and he welcomed it with open arms.

* * * * *

A fire at Sacred Heart! It couldn't be. Danuta searched her mind. Had she somehow managed to set a fire at the church? Yes, she did stop and light a candle on her way to work. Could this have been the cause? Oh, what folly she had entertained at being relieved when she had seen her house still standing. What folly, too, that Jarvis had gone from the threat of one fire to the heart of another.

"Is that why God has sent you?" she said to the beautiful apparition.

But the beautiful apparition didn't answer right away. Because he had just realized who he was talking to. The Polack's pretty wife, the one the fight had started over.

Tyler, now that Leszek knew where he was living, thought it best to seek new lodgings. He was just on his way to the Queen of Heaven parish on the other end of the neighborhood when he bumped into Danuta.

When the apparition hesitated in his reply, Danuta moved on, but Tyler ran after her.

"I told you, there's a fire. Go home."

"Did God send you to mock me?"

"No."

"Why then?"

"God didn't send me."

"Who then?"

"I was just walking down the street, that's all."

"Did you see an old man and a child at the church?"

"No," said Tyler, who wanted to add that he *had* seen her husband. But how could he explain why he knew it was her husband?

"Are you sure?"

"I didn't see them," said Tyler. And, even if he had looked, he would not have seen them. Jarvis and Sandra were both peacefully asleep, stretched out on the hard pews.

"What were you doing there?"

"Me? Well . . . I live there."

"So the church has a real angel."

"I'm not an angel."

"Then what are you?"

"A man."

"To be so beautiful, is it a blessing or a curse?" Danuta yelled as she ran.

"What do you think?" Tyler replied, running beside her.

* * * * *

Norma was, despite her recent bout of smoke inhalation, smoking her first cigarette in many years—a habit she'd given up when Julio, as a child, had fallen prey to public service announcements. When she couldn't take the boy's nagging anymore, Norma threw away her cigarettes—an ultimate sacrifice, since the habit was a source of great comfort in her burdensome life.

But here she was smoking. That's the thing about the habit, it never lets you go, she thought. Even when you go years without a cigarette, the desire is still there, catching you unaware. It's as if your body wants to safely feel as if it's on fire. To see smoke coming from the nose, the mouth, yet not be consumed.

Norma hadn't succumbed during Julio's years in the gang, hadn't given in after she'd been deposited on the shore by the Saints, hadn't yielded to the urge when either of her parents had died. But here she was caving in after all this time. And why? Because she had fallen in love and she was scared to death.

Norma had been in love twice before—both disasters. With her husband, a boy she had married in her native village when she was just seventeen, and with a man she had met at work when she was in her mid-thirties.

Norma's husband had abandoned her and the boy shortly after their arrival in Chicago. Factory worker by day, flamenco guitarist by night, the man was resentful of his life as a laborer, had grand delusions of becoming the next Segovia, and one day simply decided to take off and pursue his dream. Norma had never heard from him again. Although once she thought she saw him singing in the subway.

As for the man at work, well, it was an old story. A man in an unhappy marriage, from which he promised Norma he was trying to extricate himself. But it was not so easy, there were the children. Besides, he, like Norma, was a Catholic. It was difficult to get an annulment when you have four children. Also, the man was an Anglo. A different background, different customs, a different way of thinking, a different language spoken in the head. He was also five years younger than Norma, had a good position, and came from a wealthy family. Ay, ay, ay. What a mess it had been. She had been crazy with love for the man. Obsessed. She did not know herself. What pain, what suffering she had endured for the three years it had lasted. The lies, the secrets, the late-night telephone calls. The scenes, the tears, the feeling that her body were being torn in pieces.

After it ended and Norma returned to sanity, she vowed never again would she engage in such foolishness. Except for love for family and love for friends and love for God, she would have no part of it. Never.

* * * * *

The fire trucks were just arriving when Danuta and Tyler approached the burning church. Danuta tried to rush up the church's stone steps, but a firefighter stopped her.

"But my friend and my daughter are inside."

"We'll take care of it. Now, if you'll just step away."

"Please hurry."

"Please step aside."

Tyler, who had been standing with his back to the firefighter, suddenly turned. One glimpse of Tyler sent the firefighter screaming to the ground, and Tyler quietly slipped inside the church.

The news media had started to arrive in their vans. Father Flynn was surrounded by cameras and microphones.

"Do you suspect arson, Father?"

"Do you think it could be mafia-related, Jerry?" asked John "Hound Dog" Bludgeon, the crime syndicate reporter who liked to act as if everyone he interviewed were his personal friend.

"Have you talked to the Cardinal?"

"What ever happened to that million dollars for the repair work?"

None of the reporters seemed to be interested in Father Flynn's replies. They just kept firing questions. Jeremiah felt as if he were back in the seminary, where his superiors had buffeted him with queries about the nature of God. They, too, hadn't given Jeremiah adequate time to ponder his answers.

He just let the reporters ramble on, and looked up at his burning temple. Flames like dragons' breath were coming out of the central dome. Smoke oozed out of the cracks around the stained glass windows. A blast of heat hit him in the face. It was winter in Chicago, but here he was sweating. He felt like the bums who warmed themselves around raging trash cans. Yes, Jeremiah thought, quite a bonfire, quite a way to warm the old bones on a cold winter's night.

So, all of it had been sheer folly. His fasting, his prayers, the collection drive, the planned miracle involving Tyler, the angel-man. All of his efforts during the past year—an old man's last folly. And then Jeremiah smiled, smiled at the folly of it all, the futility of his meager attempts to foil fate, smiled at his own powerlessness, his own minuteness in the universal scheme of things.

When Jeremiah Flynn's photo appeared on the cover of the *Chicago Tribune* the next day, he was smiling broadly, the fire raging madly behind him.

CHAPTER 14

Votives

"Mr. Purcell is asking for you. He won't shut up about it. You'd better come."

"In this?" Norma asked, indicating her open-at-the-back hospital gown.

"Here, put this on like a jacket," said the nurse, passing Norma another washed-out hospital gown decorated with faded blue fleurs-de-lis.

"Hurry up. You don't want him to kick off waiting for you, do you?"

No wonder people die in hospitals, Norma thought.

In the hallway, the nurse indicated a wheel chair. "You'd better sit in this. Regulations."

After a bumper car ride in the wheel chair, with Norma's knees banging against the elevator door, they arrived at Henry's room.

"Now leave us alone," Henry barked at the nurse.

"No funny business, okay, old codger," the nurse replied, winking as she left the room.

"After dealing with her," Henry said to Norma, "I may alter my view on capital punishment."

"Always funny, huh?" Norma replied. "Always with a joke."

"Then why aren't you laughing?"

"I am. Somewhere."

Henry smiled wide, then reached for Norma's hand.

"Norma, Sacred Heart is burning."

"Yes, I know."

"I've got to be there. I've got to see what happens."

"Isn't one fire enough for one night?"

"Please, Norma, find my clothes."

"But they have put them somewhere else."

"Then find me a doctor's outfit, even a nurse's outfit . . . ."

Norma crept to the doorway and looked in both directions. Then she sneaked, unseen, into the hallway and was gone.

* * * * *

Manuel parked behind the botanica. It wasn't until he walked around to the front of the building that he noticed the black smoke against the white winter sky.

But what can be burning, he thought. I saw no omens. Then again, I have been so taken up with Emilia's obsession that I have neglected everything else.

Manuel turned a complete circle while he looked in the sky— smoke coming from all directions. He wondered why he had not noticed it before, why he had not heard the fire trucks. But his mind had been elsewhere; he had blocked out everything else.

The bells of Sacred Heart broke into his consciousness. Strange, he thought. They never ring the bells at this hour. It must be the church that's on fire.

Manuel ran the three blocks to the church, the bells tolling all the while.

When he got to the burning church, he looked up. From the bell tower, he saw his creation, Tyler, swinging from the rope that tolled the bell.

What have I done, thought Manuel. I have created this . . . this being who has gone crazy from looking at his own reflection. Now he is a lunatic who has set fire to the church. The church! Burning! It couldn't be. Never would I have believed it. Why did I not see it coming? He cursed Emilia and her dirt fetish. Cursed Leszek, his inept apprentice. If only I had been able to give Emilia's case to him, maybe I would have had time to prevent this tragic blaze.

* * * * *

While Henry waited for Norma to return, he found a sheet of paper and a pencil and began to write down questions. How did the fire start? Was it arson? Was the insurance paid up? Were there any injuries? Who was the last person in the church? How many alarms was the fire? What about that poor soul, the angel man, who lives in the bell tower? Could it have been the candles?

Henry had devoted an entire chapter of his book to candles. There was a long-standing controversy in the Chicago archdiocese about candles versus electric wicks. The Cardinal wanted to ban candles altogether, especially in the older churches. But the tradition of candle burning, especially among the ethnic communities, was just too strong. The Cardinal had capitulated, but had warned that disaster would result.

In his book, Henry had used the candle controversy as a metaphor for the two divergent camps in religion—not just the Catholics—the traditionalists and the modernists. As for himself, Henry had no particular view on the subject. He'd been brought up a Methodist, and for years had felt no tie to any particular religion.

Not an irreligious man, but certainly a nonreligious one, Henry was stunned that he had fallen so hard for Norma—a former New Age preacher, a practicing Catholic, who had been rescued by Saints.

* * * * *

Manuel once again looked up at the church. The firefighters aimed a spotlight at the bell tower. They were raising the ladder, setting the stage to rescue Tyler, who was no longer visible. Suddenly, a stiff, inert form was shoved onto the ledge. So, there he is, thought Manuel. That is why he did not come to work. And then Manuel saw Tyler in all his radiance standing behind Leszek, holding him by the shoulders. So, they have each met their fate, thought Manuel. They have found one another.

And as Manuel continued to look at the two men, they no longer seemed human. They were statues, frozen in final poses.

* * * * *

Norma, a vision in a starched nurse's uniform, stood in the doorway. She entered the room and quietly closed the door.

"Here, this is all I could find," she said, handing Henry the green shirt and pants of a maintenance worker. "I hope they're your size."

"My size or somebody else's, they're my ticket out of here."

Norma turned as Henry eased himself out of bed. Damn that nurse, she was right, he thought. I *am* dizzy. Henry held onto the bed railing to steady himself.

When Norma heard no movement, she said: "Do you need help?"

"Norma, my sweet, if we are going to get along, let's get one thing straight. I am not a helpless old man."

"I didn't think you were," she replied, smiling.

The dizziness had passed, and Henry quickly donned the worker's uniform. Here at last he was getting his wish: To be a member of the proletariat, to see how it feels to live the simple life. Henry's working-class fantasy was just kicking in when reality asserted itself.

"But I have no shoes," he said. "A barefooted maintenance man will be a red flag."

Norma looked in the closet, under the bed. Nothing.

"Here. Wear these," she said, taking off her shoes.

Henry tried them on. "They fit," he said, not really surprised.

"Lucky for you I wore flats today," said Norma.

"Lucky for me," he said, hugging her good-bye.

"Lucky for you we have the same size feet."

"I'm sure we'll find we have many things in common," he said, blowing her a kiss from the doorway.

Norma stood at the window and watched for Henry. As she waited for him to appear, she worried: But he has no coat, no socks, no hat. What if he is apprehended on his way out? What if he is not well enough to leave?

As she stood waiting, feeling the cold tile on her bare feet, Norma felt like praying. Praying for Henry, praying for Sacred Heart, praying for Julio, who was probably at the fire.

No, thought Norma. The last thing I need right now is another disaster.

CHAPTER 15

The Fool's Journey

When Leszek came out of shock, the sights he saw, the feelings he felt were enough to send him right back into a stupor.

His mind started to race. What am I doing, standing on the ledge of this bell tower, looking down on a crowd? There's Danuta crying, holding Sandra, also crying, pointing up at me. There is Jarvis, as always, making notes, perhaps writing a poem about the blaze. And the heat, the flames! What happened? And who is this holding onto my shoulders?

Leszek tried to turn around, but the hands held him fast, as if he were in a vise.

And, here, the firemen raising the ladder. How did I get here? What happened?

Leszek's recent shock had produced one merciful side effect— partial amnesia. He had completely forgotten about his trip to the church to set Tyler on fire. The scene of the man's burning body and resurrection were totally erased from Leszek's mind. He was experiencing a highly-selective form of amnesia that had wiped every trace of Tyler from his consciousness. Leszek had forgotten about the fight at the mini-mart, the curse, the encounter with his own double, even his apprenticeship with Manuel.

But, like most amnesiacs, Leszek had the feeling that he was forgetting something. Something important. Something he should remember.

He screwed his eyes shut and tried to remember. But how can I remember, he thought. The fire, the family below, the firemen, the stranger whose hands are gripping me.

Still, Leszek tried. In his mind, he went back to the last thing he remembered—the burnt toast at breakfast. Yes, he remembered that burnt toast. He could even smell it. But, perhaps it was just the burning church. The bread wrapper had boasted of high fiber, and Leszek had heard on the radio that they put wood shavings in the dough. When the toast burned, it smelled like a burning building. And how this burning building smelled like his blackened breakfast.

No, he thought, I must remember something else. Something important. What was the last thing that happened? Something of consequence. He remembered Danuta putting on her white nurse's pantyhose before leaving for work. He remembered the bleached smell of her uniform as she bent to kiss him good-bye.

But how did I get here? Why did I come here? Once again, he tried to free himself from the hands of the unknown person behind him. If I know who it is, maybe I will remember what happened. But, no use. The man—Leszek assumed it had to be a man; if it were a woman, he would die of shame—was too powerful.

* * * * *

Henry had no money, no identification, no coat, no socks, and no hat. Just a thin shirt, thin pants, and Norma's shoes. He wasn't even wearing underwear. At long last, his fantasy had been fulfilled. He was a man of the street.

It was about a mile and a half to the church. Snow was falling. A wind like icy knives was blowing, and Henry was walking right into it. The fire was still raging. Henry could see the black smoke rising.

As he walked, Henry saw others walking in the direction of the fire—like moths to a flame, human beings can't resist a fire, he thought. The primal instinct to look in the flames. As if man were still amazed at the discovery of the element, as wondrous before it as the cavemen had been.

The cold and wind and snow had not taken the edge off of Henry's tendency toward philosophizing. On the contrary, his bodily discomfort seemed to mobilize all his senses. He was acutely aware of everything around him: the sounds of passing cars, the gentle drifting of the snowflakes, the yellow glow of the streetlights. It seemed to Henry that everything was outlined in starker relief, like a painting by Roualt.

In the warm comfort of the hospital room, Henry's head had been dull, his body sluggish. But now he found new energy, a new sense of purpose. It isn't conscience, it's *comfort* that makes cowards of us, he thought. It's easy for me to think this, he mused. I have a Lake Shore Drive apartment and a bloated bank account. He laughed. What a fool I am. What an old fool.

* * * * *

Leszek looked down. The firemen were having trouble with the ladder. He looked around at the crowd. He saw a Latino waving at him, yelling something, which Leszek could not hear. The Latino was pointing wildly at the man who held Leszek. What is he trying to tell me, Leszek thought. Who is holding me in this burning church? Could God Himself have come down from heaven to do this? A Saint? An angel?

An angel . . . an angel. Somewhere at the back of Leszek's mind something was loosening up. What he had forgotten had something to do with an angel. Still, Leszek could not remember.

"Who's there?" Leszek yelled, the alternating heat of the fire and cold of the winter night making his body shake and his voice quiver.

The man did not answer, but merely tightened his grip.

"Who is it?" Leszek implored.

No reply.

"What do you want?"

The man didn't answer.

Leszek's words rang a bell in his mind. WHO'S THERE? WHO IS IT? WHAT DO YOU WANT? He had heard these words recently. When? Where? Why?

But Tyler remembered when, where, and why. Unlike Leszek, he had full access to his memories. Yes, he remembered uttering the words in the darkness as Leszek crept up to set him on fire. And now here was his foe speaking the same lines.

Tyler had returned to the bell tower to save Leszek. He had rung the bell to capture the firefighters' attention. He was holding the man in place so he would not panic and run into the burning church. But now that he remembered so vividly what this man had done to him, he felt like shoving him from the bell tower to the street below. Killed, smashed like a bug right in front of the horrified faces of his family.

* * * * *

Henry thought of the time he'd had Katie York, the psychic, on his program. She'd read his Tarot cards right on the air. The only thing he remembered about it was the Fool card, which seemed to play a central role in the reading.

Later, he'd looked up the card in a book. A young lad looks out into the distance, not seeing the precipice that lies before him. With another step, he may tumble into the realm of matter. He holds a white rose—as symbol of spiritual desires. Over his shoulder he carries the Wand of Will, from which hangs a wallet containing the four elements—Fire, Water, Air, and Earth—which he will use on his journey. At his feet, a small dog prances to show that though the youth's ideals are lofty, the life of the senses will also accompany him on his journey.

* * * * *

Seeing Leszek's sorrowful wife had sparked a heroic impulse in Tyler. He had ridden that noble impulse right up to the point where the man had uttered the lines that reminded Tyler of his recent pain and suffering. Pain and suffering that would continue, now that he was more beautiful than ever.

Where will I go? Nowhere. What will I do? Nothing. There was nothing to do except stay in the burning church and end his life. But even that won't work, he thought. I am invulnerable to fire. Perhaps drowning, then. I'll jump in the lake. But, no, that would probably fail, as well. Tyler had read the newspaper accounts of Sister Angelina's rescue. If Saints saved her, he thought, angels will come for me. I will never be able to escape this curse.

While musing, Tyler had loosened his grip on Leszek, who quickly freed himself and turned to face his captor.

* * * * *

The journey. Yes, thought Henry as he moved closer to the fire. That's what we so easily forget. That it's a journey. Not a destination. And I'm still travelin', maybe a little slower, but, pals, I'm still movin' on. Henry's private thoughts often echoed the folk songs he frequently played on his program.

The cold raged, but Henry's arms were at his sides. "Come into me, Cold!" he thought. An old trick he had once learned from a yogi. Don't resist, invite it in, and it will have no power over you. Henry knew that if he wrapped his arms around himself, he would start to shiver and feel the cold. "Come into me, Cold! Here I am! Come and get me!" Henry laughed the liberated laugh of the fool.

So here it is, he thought. He stood on the corner and watched the fire. Now the controversy would end, Henry thought. It was all over.

* * * * *

"You!" Leszek said, remembering it all in a flood.

"Yes, me!" Tyler replied.

Leszek took a step backward to put some distance between himself and the man. He came precariously close to the edge. The crowd below screamed.

"Just answer me one thing," said Tyler.

"What?" rasped Leszek.

"How did you know it was me?"

And, against all logic, Leszek barked out a loud laugh. Can it be, he thought, can it be that the man does not know?

"Let me in on the joke."

"You do not know?"

"Know what?"

"That after what happened at the mini-mart, I put a curse on you."

Ah. That felt good, thought Leszek. Despite the dire circumstances — the fire, the grieving family, the face-to-face meeting with his adversary — Leszek felt unbounded relief. He had confessed.

"You did this to me?"

"I had help."

"I thought I did it, by wishing for beauty."

"Well, then, you got your wish," said Leszek, who burst into a fit of giggling.

"So, if you put the curse on me, you can take it off. Take it off! Now! I want to be the way I was before."

"I don't know how to take it off."

"Then the one who helped you . . . ."

"He won't reverse the curse."

"Why not?"

"It is not something Manuel would do."

"Have you asked him?"

"Well . . . no."

"Then ask him."

Leszek turned and motioned to Manuel, who understood.

What a waste, Manuel thought. It was one of my best efforts.

PART TWO:

JUDGEMENT DAY

CHAPTER 16

The Reversal

As Leszek waited for rescue, Tyler slipped into the burning heart of the church. He ran through the flames, leaping through gaps in the building where stairways and landings had once been. He looked up as the church dome began to split. As he watched, flames engulfed the painting of Jesus pointing to His Sacred Heart. The Sacred Heart went up in a burst of fire, then crashed to the ground in a hail of falling plaster.

When Tyler walked through a doorway to the balcony and looked down to see no floor below him, he felt a motor start to whir in the area of his solar plexus. Then he was flying. Plaster fell, statues toppled, walls collapsed, and Tyler breezed through the disaster.

He started to feel something. Something strange. He didn't know how to put a name to it. He felt light, buoyant. He was smiling. Disaster all around him, but it didn't matter. He felt . . . what? He had never felt this before. What did you call this feeling? And then he remembered the name. Something he had heard about but had never experienced. Joy. That was it. Pure joy.

* * * * *

Manuel hurried back to the botanica. He felt deeply torn about reversing the curse on Tyler. This was a serious thing, to destroy an artistic creation. In Manuel's mind, the act was tantamount to his beloved Pablo Neruda burning a manuscript of unpublished poetry.

But I am no fool, he thought. I know when to give in. To go on would be folly. I must bite the bullet.

But this was no ordinary case. Manuel had never had such a stunning success. Never before had he produced such a magnificent creation. And, to be honest, he wasn't quite sure how he had managed it. Had there been just the right mix of the planets, the phase of the moon, plus the man's own desire, coupled with Manuel's spell that had generated such an extraordinary result? If so, where were the planets tonight? Where was the moon? Where was the angel-man's own desire? Manuel felt that he would need all the help he could get to return the angel-man to the unfortunate creature he had once been.

* * * * *

After the ladder was in place, a firefighter yelled over a megaphone for Leszek to wait for rescue. But Leszek, in a high state of elation, saw no need. He hopped onto the ladder and began his descent from the burning church.

As he climbed down each rung, Leszek's heart grew lighter and lighter. I have confessed to my enemy, he thought. I have asked the Mexican to reverse the curse. My family is waiting for me. I have been saved from the fire.

Suddenly, Leszek felt the ladder start to shake, then tremble, then vibrate so fiercely that he felt as if he were inside a motor. He tried to look down to see the source of the shaking, but his vision was blurred by the movement, and it was all he could do just to hold on.

The shaking was so violent that Leszek feared that his very soul would come loose and go shooting into the void. But all at once the shaking stopped, and Leszek felt as if he were floating peacefully on the ocean. Ah, how calm he felt. Now, he thought, only a few steps back to earth.

But when he looked down, there was nothing but the black night beneath his feet. The ladder had come loose from its moorings and was sailing through space.

Leszek hung on for dear life.

* * * * *

It would have been difficult to reverse the curse under the best of circumstances. But Manuel was under pressure to perform the work quickly. He didn't know whether this was good or bad. It was good in the sense that his rational mind would have to get out of the way — there was no time for conscious planning. But even the imagination requires time to do its work. And that's the commodity that Manuel lacked — sheer minutes and hours and days to allow his unconscious to play with the problem.

So he forged ahead. He used all of his best supplies. There was no talcum in the alum, no tallow in the candles. He even unwrapped the ancient prayer book that he had received from his mentor. And he used his last precious drops of holy water from the Santa Barbara church in Mexico City.

Manuel worked. Herbs burned, beeswax candles blazed, incantations filled the room. "Give the man his desire," Manuel intoned. "Let him be as he wishes to be."

* * * * *

When Danuta saw the ladder break free and start to ascend into space, she was not surprised. She had been waiting for a personal tragedy to occur, and now it had happened.

As the crowd gasped and pointed to the sky, as the TV cameras rolled, as the photos flashed, as pencils scratched across notebooks, as the firefighters lit cigarettes with shaking hands, Danuta held her mouth in a firm hard line and said: "My fault."

Amid the noise and confusion, Jarvis didn't hear her. He felt completely helpless at his inability to comfort Barbara and Sandra. What could he do? What could he say? Poor Les had flown away, up into the sky on a ladder.

Back on the bench, Jarvis had always had a precedent to fall back on. But there was no precedent for this.

Wait. Maybe there *was* a precedent. Something in the Bible. Like most Catholics, Jarvis was fuzzy on the Old Testament. But he vaguely remembered something. He searched his mind. A, no. B, no. C, no. D, no. E, no. F, no. G, no. H, no. I, no. J, no. K, no. L, no. Wait, go back. Something with a J. Jeremiah, no. Joshua, no. Jerome, no—no Jerome in the Old Testament. The twin, who was the twin? Jacob. Yes. Jacob and the ladder.

Jarvis ran up to Father Flynn. "What happened to Jacob?"

"Jacob who?"

"In the Bible."

"Please, Sir, my church is burning, a man has just disappeared on a ladder, I have no time . . . ."

"Jacob and the ladder—what happened? Tell me. It's a precedent. It will help."

"There were angels. It was a dream, I think. It's been a while."

Angels. Yes, that's it. But what happened? And, since they were standing before a burning Catholic church, and not a Protestant one, none of the bystanders sported a Bible.

Jarvis ran to a pay phone and dialed the librarian he called regularly to check obscure references for the epic poem, *Judgement Day*, he had been working on for months.

"Reference desk."

"Jarvis here. Quick. The Old Testament. Jacob and the ladder. Read it to me."

"How's the poem coming?"

"Fine. Please hurry."

"Relax, it's just a poem."

"I'm in a pay phone. Please . . . ."

"It's not like there haven't been thousands, millions of poems written already. Take it easy."

"Miss Eichenbacher, I am in desperate straights here. Please read me the verse."

"I'm looking, okay?"

"I don't mean to be rude. But the church is on fire and a dear friend just flew up in the sky on a ladder . . . ."

"What an imagination you poets have. Okay. Here it is. Ready?"

"Read it."

"Got your pen and paper handy?"

"I'm ready. Please tell me what it says."

"Here goes. *And he dreamed, and behold a ladder set up on the earth, and the top of it reached to heaven: and behold the angels of God ascending and descending it. And behold, the Lord stood above it and said, I am the Lord God of Abraham thy father, and the God of Isaac . . . .*"

"That's enough," said Jarvis and hung up.

As he walked back to join Barbara and Sandra, he thought: Les is in for a rough night.

* * * * *

Manuel should have been more specific. He should have asked that Tyler be returned to his former state of ugliness. For at the moment that Manuel asked the spirits to give the man his desire, Tyler was caught up in a wave of flying omnipotence where his desire was to be not the old Tyler—but God Himself.

CHAPTER 17

The Jester

As Julio held the hose and doused the fire, Hector Fernandez and a few of his hangers-on jeered at him from the sidelines.

"Seen Santa Maria lately, Julio?"

"Look up Our Lady's skirt, Villalobos?"

"Had any wet dreams about the Madonna?"

As Julio struggled to hold the hose in place while the water rushed through at high pressures, he had to fight the urge to turn and aim at Hector and his cohorts.

But he took a deep breath and concentrated on his task. He watched as the flames died out one by one. He had power over the fire, he didn't need to prove himself to a bunch of sad cases who would never feel powerful about anything. Besides, they had seen the Virgin themselves. Why were they acting as if he had made it all up?

"How's your girlfriend, Guadalupe, Julio?"

"Hey, Juan Diego, where's your roses?" said Hector, laughing merrily and elbowing his compatriots. Hector deemed himself a mighty wit and had spent the past several months mustering up the courage to take the stage at an open mike session in a nearby comedy club. Hector made a mental note to add a Juan Diego joke to his act. The poor peasant who had received red roses from the Virgin in the dead of winter—there was sure to be a joke there.

"Roses are red, your dick is blue, see what working in the cold will do," Hector yelled to Julio, and doubled over in a hysterical fit.

"What did the mama cucaracha say to the baby cucaracha?" asked Hector to his straight man, Fernando Diaz.

"What?" asked Fernando, right on cue.

"The mama cucaracha says: 'You're drivin me crazy, kid. You're makin me *climb the walls.*'" Hector paused and then looked around, not just at his buddies, but at the entire assembly of fire watchers, firefighters, and media types. "Get it?" he said with a broad smile. When he didn't get a laugh—worse, when he was greeted by quizzical looks—he turned to Fernando and said: "Some people just don't got a sense of humor."

Jesus, thought Julio, and to think I spent the greater part of my life with those guys.

Henry witnessed Hector's performance and started to make some notes. *Fires attract jesters. Perhaps the element needs some relief from its own intensity. Yes, the fire says, I bring destruction, maiming, death; but I also bring warmth, life, and light. I'm out of control now, so I need something to put everything back into perspective. How about a few jokes, folks? How about a little fiddling, a little dancing through the flames? Come on, people, lighten up.*

* * * * *

Jarvis wasn't wrong about Leszek being in for a rough night. The angels had already appeared. Tiny little cherub angels, like Christmas tree ornaments, danced up and down the ladder, singing *Ave Maria* in high-pitched voices that sounded like Alvin and the Chipmunks.

The angels darted back and forth at fast speeds. Their size, their quick movements, and their high voices made Leszek feel as if he were dodging rats. He jumped involuntarily, and when he tried to place his feet back on the rungs, they went right through—until he was straddling the ladder like a see-saw. The tiny angels glided right over him, their footsteps feeling like bites from rats' tiny teeth.

The ladder was shooting straight up into the night sky. Leszek wondered where he was headed. Around and around the globe forever? To the moon? The North Pole? Back to Poland? Worse, to Siberia? Perhaps he would land on a small Pacific island and spend the rest of his days spear fishing. No, he was headed north, headed upward.

He thought back to his climb from the burning church. He had been so elated, so relieved. He had been just a few steps from earth—the ladder, a bridge taking him to safety. But the ladder wasn't taking him to safety anymore. It was propelling him to God-only-knew where.

* * * * *

"So, I'm walking down the street, and this guy comes up to me and says: 'How do I get home from here?' So I says: 'Where do you live?' So he says: 'Why do you wanna know? You gonna rob me?'" Even Hector's compadres looked puzzled when he finished delivering this one.

Though the crowd wasn't laughing at Hector's lame jokes, things had, in fact, lightened up. The sense of dread and doom had been replaced by a serene acceptance. So be it. We'll start over. We'll do better. We'll put in decent wiring next time.

"Yeah, man, I stopped at the *Roadkill* Cafe the other night. What a meal! I had the chicken that *didn't* cross the road."

Groans from the crowd. Hector interpreted this as progress.

"So, see, there was this rabbi, this priest, and this minister, and they . . . " Before Hector could finish, Julio turned and blasted him with the water. Hector felt as if he had been shot. He was sure that the hard stream of water had made a hole right through his body. He fell to the ground, holding his heart.

Julio ran over to give him another shot with the pressurized water. But, before he could, the hose pulled from his hands and started to rise into the air like a snake charmed by a flute. The hose rose higher and higher, danced, spun, and sprayed the crowd in every direction.

Then the hose turned on Julio and chased him into the night.

* * * * *

When Henry saw Tyler emerge from the dying church, a phrase popped into his mind: *Ye are gods and all ye are children of the most high.*

Where had it come from, Henry wondered. It had been years since he had read the Bible. He would have to look up the passage later in *Strong's Concordance*.

Tyler stood with his arms outstretched. The remains of the church smoldered behind him. He took a step into the crowd. The mass of people recoiled in fear. Tyler took another step forward, and the people took a step backward. Then Tyler started to walk briskly, his hands beckoning, imploring the people. At this, the people turned tail and started running.

Even the firefighters had to fight the urge to flee. Instead, they took their tools and entered the charred shell of the church to find the source of the fire.

Henry, who had the benefit of blurred vision, was the only one able to look at Tyler. He watched as Tyler surveyed the ruins. When new onlookers arrived, Tyler moved toward them to deliver the words that were forming in his head. But as soon as the people got a glimpse of Tyler, they seemed to evaporate into the night.

No one will listen, Tyler thought. Suddenly he felt a tap on his shoulder. Tyler turned and saw Henry, notebook and pencil poised.

"Well, angel-man, I see you made it out in one piece."

"Something happened in there. During the fire."

"Let me in on it."

"I turned into a god. I can fly now. And there are all these words swirling around in my head."

"So you think you're a god, huh?"

"I know I am."

"How do you know?"

"I just know."

"Omniscient, huh?"

"I know everything."

"What else?"

"I think I'm all-powerful, too. But I have to try it out."

"What are you gonna do?"

"Something big, I think . . . ."

"Do me a favor, okay?"

"What's that?"

"Make sure I'm around when you do it."

"For your book?"

"You see right through me."

"It's too late for books."

"How's that?"

The mass of thoughts formed into words in Tyler's mind. Then he spoke them aloud: "THE DAY OF JUDGEMENT IS AT HAND."

CHAPTER 18

The Milky Way

Tyler didn't know where he was flying, but when he got there it seemed like the destination of a well-thought-out plan. He was home—his former home. The place where Deeanna, Charlie, and Eva lived. He recognized his building by the large painted letters—WHVN-FM—on the side of the roof that faced the elevated tracks. Snow was falling, but the top half of the letters could still be seen.

Now it was time to land. Tyler was still a little shaky in that area. His inner navigator told him to slow down, then he straightened out his body and descended slowly to the ground. A perfect landing. Hells bells, I've really got a knack for this, Tyler thought.

He entered the hallway, walked up a flight, then reached in his pocket. His keys were there. Strange, after all he'd been through, that he'd remembered to carry his keys. But then again he'd always had an affinity for keys. He was always finding keys, the way some people were always losing keys. At his apartment, he had a cigar box full of them. Lord only knew what they opened. Safe deposit boxes, motel rooms, mailboxes, bus lockers, garages, and houses. Somewhere out there, there were locks that all of the keys fit.

When they'd gotten divorced, Deeanna had demanded that Tyler return the house keys. But he would have been no more able to do that than he would have been able to cut out a piece of his own heart. The keys were more than just keys to him. They held part of his life. All the times he had opened the door: returning from work, from church, from the doctor with Charlie, from the hospital when the kids were born. No, he could not return the house keys. He'd told her he'd lost them. She called him a liar and then called a locksmith.

So even though the locks had been changed, Tyler still tried his key. If this one didn't work, he'd return to his apartment, grab the cigar box, and stand there and try all the keys until he found one that fit.

But when he touched the key to the lock, the door breezed open. Why would they leave the door unlocked? At this time of night? In this neighborhood?

Tyler walked into the darkened living room and sat on the sofa. It was lucky he could light his own way. Deeanna had rearranged the furniture, had even added a few straggly items. In the pitch dark, he may have tripped and awakened his family. And he didn't want them to wake up until he had a few moments to think, to collect himself, to figure out why he was there.

* * * * *

Only a year, Norma thought. Only a year since I went to see the faith healer who still haunts my dreams—Sister Merlina Talbott. And look at what has happened since. I've done things I never thought I would do. Smoking. Falling in love. Leading a double life, starting a religion. My family—strangers to me. And now this. I have hit bottom.

As the hospital elevator descended, Norma looked down at her stolen shoes. Her feet felt hot and cold at the same time. They were sweating so much that she feared she'd made a sloshing, vacuumy sound when she stepped from the elevator.

And the woman she had stolen them from—the appendectomy with the kind husband who had given Norma the package of cigarettes. How could she steal at all, let alone from such nice people? What is happening to me? I'm not myself. Why risk hell, when the shoes are not even my style—not even my size.

But Norma needed to get out of the hospital quickly. There was no time to ask the attendants to find her a pair of shoes—besides, how would she explain where hers had gone? There was no time to search the hospital, to poke around until she found a stranger's shoes. No, she had to take what was easily available.

A true Catholic, Norma realized it was far easier to ask for forgiveness than permission. She would find out the woman's name and address and would send her a new pair. She would go to Confession and admit her sin. But, until this recompense had been made, Norma was carrying a mortal sin on her soul.

Even this did not deter her. She needed to find Henry. Needed to find him right away. She had a bad feeling that something was wrong. And, since praying was fraught with such danger for Norma, the only thing she could do was take the matter into her own hands.

Norma's valuables had been locked away by the hospital staff. She had no wallet, no money. She was wearing a stolen nurse's uniform and stolen athletic shoes—ones that made her ankles feel thick, her legs stocky. She felt ugly in the shapeless uniform, ugly in the bulky shoes. Her makeup was caked and her mascara was in clumps that kept falling on her cheeks. Her lipstick was long gone.

She was torn. She knew she had to find Henry. But she didn't want him to see her like this. *Santa Maria, I don't even have my keys, or I'd run home and do a five-minute makeover. Who would love me the way I am now? Still, I must not think of myself, I must think of helping, no, not helping—he would not like that—finding Henry.*

* * * * *

It had been months now since Tyler had seen his children. God only knew what Deeanna had told them. Sure, he had called. Sure, he had made up a story, but Deeanna had not been convinced. Nothing had ever deterred Tyler from his weekly visitations. What was going on? Was he in jail? Drinking? With another woman?

Tyler had told her that he'd taken a job in the Alaskan oil fields and, when he had saved enough money, he would come back. Deeanna wanted to know why he wasn't sending money in the meantime. He said he wouldn't get paid until the job was over. Meanwhile, Tyler told her to take out a personal loan to tide them over.

But now he was being drawn back, despite the change in his appearance. What would he say to them? Who would he say he was?

He walked into the kitchen, found a pen and paper, and started to write a note. Before he could finish, he heard someone shuffling down the hallway. Where could he—a radiant, glowing being—hide? As Tyler was reaching for the back doorknob, he heard Charlie's voice.

"Daddy," he said.

Tyler turned, and the child, the poor child, with his jerking movements and unfortunate resemblance to the old Tyler, walked over to him.

"I missed you, Daddy."

"What makes you think I'm your Daddy?" Tyler said, holding back a sob.

"You look like my Daddy."

Tyler's heart leapt. My God, maybe I've turned back, he thought. He touched the boy's shoulders, then raced into the bathroom and looked at himself in the mirror. He was still beautiful, even more beautiful than the last time he'd looked. But the boy had recognized him. How?

Heart pounding, Tyler plodded back to the kitchen, where his son was trying valiantly to pour himself a glass of milk.

"Like some help?" Tyler whispered.

"Okay," said Charlie.

Tyler took the gallon jug from his son's jerking hands. In his time at the mini-mart, Tyler had handled thousands of gallons of milk. All that milk, he thought, feeding all those babies, poured over all that cereal, added to all that coffee. As he poured the glass of milk for his son, Tyler had a vision of himself as the Cosmic Milkman, the great nourisher. He saw himself as huge, a giant in the sky, dressed the way milkmen did in the old days—spiffy white outfit, tidy hat. In his hand was a ladle from which milk poured endlessly. On earth, people stood with their mouths open, waiting to be fed, like baby birds.

Tyler snapped out of it and handed the milk to Charlie.

"Straw," Charlie said. "Remember?"

Tyler nodded and pulled a straw out of the cabinet, then placed it in Charlie's glass.

"Drink," Tyler said. "From your father, the milkman."

Charlie laughed, then placed his mouth to the straw and pulled. He drank without stopping, without taking a breath, just guzzled it all down, until the straw made burping noises in the empty glass.

Charlie sighed, then his whole body went limp. He smiled. It was the first time in years that he'd had any relief from his unwanted movements.

Tyler held his breath, afraid to hope that what he was seeing were true. The boy had been healed by a glass of milk from his father. Tyler had succeeded where the doctors and even Sister Merlina Talbott had failed. His son was whole again.

I can fly and I can heal people, thought Tyler. I guess I am a god now. I got my wish again.

"Daddy," Charlie said, interrupting Tyler's thoughts.

"Yes, son?"

"I'm okay now."

Tyler held the boy tight; neither spoke. The boy fell into a peaceful sleep in Tyler's arms. And, after Tyler had tucked him safely into bed—miraculously, without waking Deeanna or Eva—he stepped silently out of his former home.

He knew what he had to do next.

* * * * *

Norma started to walk, taking the same path Henry had walked an hour earlier. Like him, she was cold—freezing, in fact. Like him, she was wearing someone else's shoes. Despite the ripping cold, despite her distress about her appearance, despite her concern for Henry, Norma laughed.

Yes, she thought, here I am a middle-aged woman, and for the first time in my life I am walking a mile in someone else's shoes. Is this what the saying means? She looked around, but saw no one, so she indulged herself. She laughed until tears rolled down her cheeks, until her eyes were practically glued together with her crumbling mascara. Don't judge someone, Mama used to say, until you have walked a mile in their zapatos.

The events of the day—of the whole year, really—the stress, the strain, the uncertainty made Norma particularly susceptible to a fit of hysterics. She laughed and laughed, doubled over, put her arms across her stomach, barked, cackled, hyperventilated, nearly passed out, once again, from a lack of oxygen.

She looked down at the shoes and started laughing even harder. I'm walking a mile in the ugliest shoes that ever belonged to someone else, she thought.

Norma was all set to indulge in another belly laugh, but what she saw made her suddenly, completely sober.

A glowing, radiant being gazed down at her from the sky. Norma fell to her knees. Just my luck, she thought. On Judgement Day, I have a mortal sin on my soul. Worse still, I am wearing ugly shoes and no makeup. I will look like this for all eternity.

CHAPTER 19

Take a Letter, Maria

The massive water hose chased Julio into the dark side streets. He kept turning to see if the hose were still following him, but each time Julio looked he got a blast of icy water in the face. The hose had long since broken free from the hydrant; but, like Elisha's oil bottle, it never ran dry.

Julio didn't know why he was being chased and rained on by the ghost who had taken possession of the fire hose. He didn't understand the workings of ghosts and no longer even tried.

The only time Julio had ever been thrown off by an apparition was when the Virgin of Guadalupe had appeared at Sacred Heart. Julio still could not think of the incident without feeling as if his knees were exploding.

Without turning to see if the ghost were still pursuing him, Julio ran into the Round-the-Clock Donut Shoppe, sat down, and laid his head on the counter.

"Can I help you?" said a woman's voice.

"In a minute," Julio replied, not looking up.

"Coffee?" the woman asked.

"Later."

"Rough night?"

Why is it, Julio thought, that people never get the hint when you don't want to be bothered? They just keep yapping. He gave the woman no reply. Of course he'd had a rough night. Jesus, just look at him. Covered with soot and sweat. His face literally an icy mask from all the water the ghost had aimed at him. He was cold, scared, trembling. And, worst of all, on the verge of tears. How could he ever again feel secure in his macho persona if he wept in public?

What I need, Julio thought, is a wife. Someone I can go to when I feel this way. A home and a family.

With his external landmarks—the church and the radio station—gone, Julio, in an effort to master the dire circumstances, began to plan his future.

I'll find a good woman, have some kids, buy a house.

"Ready for that coffee yet?"

Dios mio! Jesu Christo! Santa Maria! Is this woman's soul made of ice? Can't she see what I'm going through?

"No," was all that Julio said.

Suddenly, Julio remembered about his mother in the hospital. He knew he should call to check up. But, like most sons with strong mothers, he thought Norma was invulnerable. He figured she had already reorganized the hospital's linen closets and filing system. He would call later.

"Special today. Chocolate long johns. Two for a dollar."

Julio groaned. Was this what it was like in hell? Your thoughts constantly interrupted.

"I said later, okay?" he replied, his head still on the counter, his eyes still closed.

"We've also got bran muffins. High fiber, with raisins and nuts."

"I'll let you know when I'm ready. Please, now leave me alone."

"Is the fire out?"

"Yes, yes, the fire is out."

"I still see smoke."

God, who is this woman? Who could possibly be so rude, so insensitive?

Julio opened his eyes and looked up. Oh no, he thought, recognizing her. This really tops off my night. Julio's head hit the counter. Right before he passed out cold, he thought: "Ave Maria."

* * * * *

Ever since his childhood in the slums of Warsaw, Leszek had been terrified of rats. His worst nightmare was that Danuta would learn of this cowardly streak. That one day a rat would appear in the house, she would be standing screaming on the sofa, pointing to a corner of the room, and, instead of killing the rat with a club, he would join her on the divan.

But here was something even worse. Tiny angels that moved and sounded and felt like rats—running over his body. Only minutes had passed—perhaps only seconds—but Leszek knew he could stand no more. He loosened his grip on the ladder and prayed that he would mercifully drop into the void.

"You wish for death?" he heard a deep, rich voice say.

"Yes! Yes!" Leszek screamed.

"Such a small thing would make you wish for death?"

"To me it is not small."

"You cannot run from fear."

"I can!"

"You can never run fast enough."

Leszek knew this was true. The most you could hope was to stay one step ahead. And even this was an exhausting occupation.

"How then?" he asked, not knowing to whom he was speaking.

"Welcome it."

"How?"

"Invite it in. Then it will have no power over you."

"Who are you?" Leszek asked, looking around into the blackness.

"I am your guest. Invite me in," the voice said.

"Am I in hell?" Leszek asked, vainly trying to dodge the slithering of the tiny angels.

"Invite me in, and you will see."

The ladder stopped dead. A stone gate with pillars stood before Leszek.

"Invite me in, or I will invite you."

"Come in," Leszek screamed, hoping for relief.

"Thank you. I will," said the voice.

The gate swung outward. The tiny angels stopped moving and ran through the gate. Then the gate swung shut.

Leszek leaned down and rested on the ladder. He felt totally at peace, as if nothing could ever frighten him. Leszek didn't know whether he was at the gate of heaven or the gate of hell. And he didn't care.

* * * * *

When the firefighter raised his head, Esperanza recognized him right away. Her back had been turned when he'd entered. But now when she saw his face, she remembered him as the leader of the midnight prayer society, the one who had sounded like Mickey Mouse.

And now he had passed out. What should she do? Esperanza knew she never should have told Teresa that she would fill in for her tonight. Esperanza was afraid that someone she knew would recognize her and think she'd lost her respectable job at the bank.

She had been grateful that there had been few customers. Sure, there were those big orders earlier. Take-outs for people going to watch the fires. But, mercifully, few people had stuck around to gawk at her in her pink outfit and funny hat.

This bombero must have had some night, Esperanza thought. But he seemed all right until he looked at me. The same way he looked at me in the church. Like I gave him a fright.

It is always this way with men, only more so with this one. She turned and looked at her pretty face in the mirror behind the coffee urns. Women who are fat and ugly find men to love them, she thought. But the men are afraid to come near me. And this one, the sight of me makes him faint.

This is not fair, she thought. I would rather be ugly with a man to love me than pretty with no man to love me. There is something about me that is not right. I am missing something, like a leg or an arm, only you can't see it.

What could be wrong, what could be missing? Perhaps, she thought, I have been waiting for the man to come to me. Perhaps I need to take matters into my own hands.

Esperanza knew that if she didn't stop waiting and start acting that she would be an old, alone woman. She would die without ever having felt a man's touch.

As she looked in the mirror, Esperanza could see Julio start to stir. Now is the time, she thought. I have made my resolve, now I must follow through.

She turned and moved toward Julio. He lifted his head and held it in his hands. "Ay, ay, ay," he said.

Esperanza touched his chin with her finger and tilted his face upward. She bent down to look in his eyes, which he was just bringing into focus.

"Where am I?" he asked.

"In my power," Esperanza replied, as she bent down and kissed Julio full on the mouth.

Julio felt the kiss and responded, holding his mouth to the woman's for a long moment.

But where was he? Who was he kissing? This was not Irene, or Josie, or Eugenia. No, the kiss was different. As if his body were not involved, as if he were floating in space.

He opened his eyes and gaped, horrified. "The Virgin," he rasped.

So, he can see it, Esperanza thought. But I will lie, I will make him believe it is not so. Maybe then he will want me.

"No, I am not a virgin."

"But, in the church. I saw you. You appeared."

"You do not have to be a virgin to go to church."

"But you are the Virgin of Guadalupe!"

Esperanza gasped. So, that's it, she thought.

She turned and looked at herself in the mirror. Ah, so that is why men will have nothing to do with me. I look like the Virgin of Guadalupe and they are ashamed to want me. How unfortunate for me, she thought, to look like Juan Diego's vision.

As Julio was making his way to the door, Esperanza turned and called out. "No!"

"Please," said Julio. "I must get back to the fire."

"I have a message for you," said Esperanza.

"A message?"

"Yes. Go to the Cardinal and tell him that I said he must rebuild Sacred Heart. As proof, buy a dozen red roses and say you found them growing amid the ashes of the church."

"But if you are the Lady, surely I will not have to buy the roses."

"Sometimes," she said, "you have to give miracles a little help."

CHAPTER 20

Fear and Trembling

After Tyler flew off, Henry knew he should do something. The angel-man, the god-man, or whatever he was, had said it was Judgement Day. This was important information that should be passed on somehow. But, despite the significance of the information, despite its gravity, despite its dire ramifications, the urgency that it implied, Henry still felt his thoughts drawn to his own personal concerns. He had to get back to Norma.

On his trek back to the hospital—his frozen feet fighting him every step of the way—he paused each time he saw someone on the street, and announced: "The day of judgement is at hand." Then he proceeded on his way.

Henry felt greatly satisfied at this solution to the problem. He had managed to fulfill both tasks—the cosmic and the colloquial. He was doing God's bidding and his own. How handy, he thought.

He stood in the street and stopped the passing cars. Since Henry looked so harmless, the cars slowed and people rolled down their windows. "The day of judgement is at hand," Henry yelled into the cozy warmth of the cars. And before the drivers could reply, he was once again on his way.

Henry could see the hospital in the distance. Only a block separated him from dear Normita. But as his mind was projecting ahead to scenes of warmth and safety and happiness, Henry felt something swoop down and grab him by the back of his workingman's collar. As he was being lifted into the air, Henry heard Tyler say: "Don't you know how to keep a secret?"

Ah, the road to hell, Henry mused. With all my good intentions, I have still managed to inspire the wrath of God.

Despite the doom that surely awaited him, Henry managed to remain calm. If he had learned one thing in his long and varied life, it was not to get emotional when things go bad. Anybody can weep and wail and bemoan his fate. It takes some wisdom not to fight it, to let it just wash over you, until you can think of a way out.

And Henry's mind was clicking away full tilt. Jeez Louise, Henry thought, this guy, god or no god, has really gone off half-cocked. Maybe I can talk some sense into him.

Let's see, Henry mused as the city spun below him, how should I address him? Your Highness? Your Holiness? Almighty One? Your Eminence?

"Sir," Henry began.

"No talking," Tyler replied.

"But Master . . ." Henry said.

"I told you, no talking. You've talked enough. Your radio program has been canceled," Tyler said and laughed.

Hmmm, Henry thought. Pretty smart. This guy is saying that I think life is like my talk show. Yap, yap, yap, always expecting that someone is out there listening. There's something to what he says.

Even though Henry knew he wasn't supposed to speak, there were still two words he had to say. He took the chance.

"I'm sorry," Henry said.

"You are?" Tyler replied.

"Truly," Henry said.

"All right, then," Tyler told him.

Then Tyler let go of Henry and flew away. As Henry fell, he saw his beloved city moving ever closer to him. It looked as if the entire city had been strung with Italian lights. Beautiful! What a sight! Amazing! These were Henry's thoughts as he plummeted to the ground.

* * * * *

While Julio waited, Esperanza wrote the message to the Cardinal on a napkin emblazoned with the Round-the-Clock logo—a donut with a smiling clock face. But before Julio could leave to deliver the Virgin's missive, he and the Lady heard a booming voice and ran to the door of the donut shop.

They looked around, confused. Where was the sound coming from? It was so loud, so all-pervasive, that it seemed to be coming from every direction, including the inside of their heads.

"Look," said Esperanza, pointing to the sky.

A glowing being floated by as lazily as the Goodyear blimp. In its hands was a huge trumpet.

Julio looked at the clock that smiled up at him from the Virgin's message. Words popped into his head: *Now time will be no more.*

"Do you think," said Julio, turning to his companion, "that you could talk Him out of it?"

"Me?"

"You are, after all, the Mother of God. Intercede, please."

Julio knelt down at her feet and folded his hands. This can't be Judgement Day, thought Esperanza. I'm not ready. I haven't lived. I want love. A family. A house. I want to visit the Grand Canyon. I want to see the ocean. Please God, not now. Not yet.

Despite Esperanza's spirited, though narrow, attempt at intercession, the glowing being raised the trumpet.

CHAPTER 21

Absolute Power

Not without difficulty, Jarvis had managed to convince Barbara to leave the fire. She wanted to await Les's return. But Jarvis reasoned that if Les returned they would surely receive a phone call. There was no reason to stand out in the cold with a small child in tow. Barbara acquiesced but, during each step of the walk home, threatened to turn back. Jarvis was exhausted by the time they reached their front steps.

When they entered the house, both Danuta and Jarvis were struck by the silence. For the first time, no music or talk from WHVN-FM echoed in the walls.

"The voice of heaven is no more," Jarvis said, breaking the silence. Then he carried the sleeping Sandra to her room.

Danuta stood in the darkened living room and let the silence wash over her. It was as if a friend, a bothersome friend, but a friend nonetheless, had moved without saying good-bye. Already she missed the music and the talk that used to distract her thoughts and invade her dreams. How strange, she thought, that we are never happy with the way things are. We are always looking back or looking forward, but never seeing what is now.

Danuta started to walk around the room. She paced the borders of the carpet—feeling that if she stepped off the edge, she would fall into a great nothingness.

The room was dark, except for small yellow pools cast by the streetlights outside. In one of these yellow pools, Danuta saw something that made her jump from the edge of the carpet to the sofa in one leap. There, in a corner of the room, crouched the biggest rat Danuta had ever seen. Yes, she thought, the fires have released the rats. They will all be seeking new winter homes.

She thought of crying out—but did not want to frighten her child or Jarvis, with his heart condition. They had suffered enough for one night.

She stepped down from the sofa and walked to the kitchen, where Jarvis was putting on a kettle of water.

"Tea?" he asked.

"Thank you," she replied as she reached for a tin of cookies.

"Cookies would be nice," Jarvis observed.

Danuta took the cookies and walked to the living room. The rat had not moved. She opened the front door, and placed a cookie on the threshold. Then she stepped back to see if the rat would take the bait. Danuta hoped that she could lure the rat outside, close the door, and forget all about it. She did not want to have to kill it, she did not want to have to chase it around her home. Not now. Not tonight. Two fires and a missing husband were enough.

"I feel a draft," Jarvis said, entering the room.

"Please go back into the kitchen," Danuta whispered.

"What's wrong?"

"Please make the tea. I will be right there."

Barbara rarely made any requests, so Jarvis figured she must have a good reason for asking him to leave the room. He left, but started to worry. I hope she's not becoming unbalanced from the strain. Why would she be standing there with the door wide open on a winter night? Still, Jarvis respected Barbara enough to give her the benefit of the doubt. He had done much more for repeat offenders. Didn't someone so dear to him deserve a little faith?

While Jarvis busied himself making Constant Comment tea, Danuta hid behind the sofa and watched as the rat made its way to the door. She watched intently, ready in a moment to slam the door once the rat was outside.

When the rat had nearly reached its destination, Danuta started to inch toward it. Suddenly, a large shadow loomed in the doorway. The shadow bent down, scooped up the rat, and held it up like a trophy. The huge rat wriggled and squeaked and tried to bite the shadowy hand that held it.

"I'm home," the shadow said, hurling the rat into the night.

Then the shadow took several bounding steps into the room. Danuta turned on the light, and the shadow started to develop like a Polaroid snapshot right before her eyes.

Danuta once again felt like screaming, but once again didn't want to frighten the others in the house.

First, the shadow turned bright red. Then blue washed from its feet to its head, creating a strange purple being. Next, bright yellow oozed over the surface of the shape. The three colors mixed with the shadow's own blackness, until a human form appeared. A strange man now stood in the center of the living room.

"Aren't you happy to see me?" he asked.

Danuta said nothing, just stood and stared at the stranger.

"After all I've been through, I had hoped for a warmer greeting."

* * * * *

It *is* lonely at the top, Tyler thought. Is that why God allows all this to happen down here? To break the monotony? So people will talk to Him? If everything's going okay, who prays anyway? People only pray when everything goes to hell.

Tyler wondered what he should do next. His options were limitless. He was omnipotent and omniscient. He himself was the God he was pondering. And because his vistas were so broad, so vast, he couldn't decide what to do.

It's just like at that restaurant, he thought, the one with over a hundred items on the menu. Every time I went in that place I lost my appetite trying to figure out what to order. That's the secret of McDonald's success—a few simple choices. You don't have to plumb the depths of your soul trying to decide.

Tyler realized with a jolt that this was what set God apart from men—options. The more options—the more godlike the being.

It's confusing to be God, he thought. Too many choices. Too much to think about. Who would want this job?

* * * * *

"I heard voices," Jarvis said, entering the room. He took one look at the man and dropped his hot cup of tea. "Les!" he said, stepping over the puddle of tea and the shards of Polish porcelain.

"So, someone is glad to see me," Leszek said, embracing Jarvis.

When the two men stopped hugging, they turned to face Danuta, who gave Jarvis a puzzled look.

"She's suffered a great shock tonight," Jarvis said to explain Barbara's silence. "Come on, Les, I'll make you a cup of tea."

Danuta watched them leave the room. Leszek turned and gave her a long look before he entered the kitchen. Still, she did not recognize her husband.

She sat down and tried to call up her husband's face. She tried to see his walk, the way he held a cup, a spoon. She tried to remember how he pulled on his socks, how he brushed his teeth. She tried to remember his kiss, his touch. But she could remember nothing.

This must be Leszek, she thought. Mr. Jarvis recognizes him, so it must be true. He has found his way back home.

"Leszek," she called very quietly, as a test. If he heard her, it would be a sign. If not, another kind of sign.

Leszek walked soundlessly into the room and sat next to her on the sofa.

"Yes?" he said.

"So," she answered, "I see you are no longer afraid of rats."

Leszek looked at her and laughed—a dam breaking, a great

flood of laughter. He couldn't stop. All these years, trying to hide it, and she knew all along. He grabbed Danuta and held her tight.

"That's right," he finally said, and started laughing once again.

How nice, thought Jarvis watching them from his spot in the doorway. How nice the way everything has turned out.

As Jarvis, Danuta, Leszek, and the sleeping Sandra were enjoying this moment of domestic bliss, a loud voice above them announced: *"May I have your attention, please."*

The man, the woman, and the old judge opened the door and rushed to the porch. Again, they heard it. "MAY I HAVE YOUR ATTENTION, PLEASE!"

They looked up and saw the glowing being in the night sky.

"THE TIME IS AT HAND."

CHAPTER 22
Dust Thou Art

Manuel had never felt more exhausted. It was as if the ritual had drained the very life from him. This was the first time he had ever consented to a reversal. He did not believe in reversals. Manuel believed in making choices and living with the consequences—no matter how dire. There was danger in every choice. That was just a part of living. If things could be reversed—presto!—then what was the point?

Already Manuel was regretting what he had done. He had lived his life impeccably, according to his code. And now, after all these years, he had weakened, he had succumbed to external pressure. Already, he was trying to think of a way to reverse the reversal.

Manuel sat in the darkened botanica and pondered his options. He held his head in his hands and felt the veins throbbing in his temples. He was distraught not only because he had veered from his ethical standards, not only because he had lost respect for himself, but also because he had undone the very capstone to his life's work. He, Manuel Morales, had created an angel. An angel! And, worn down by the constant demands of the dirt-eating Emilia, the sight of the burning church, and pity for his Polish apprentice, he had, in a weak moment, undone his most magnificent creation. Jesus, Maria, y Jose!

He raised his head and looked around the store. What combination of candles and powders could he use? What words could he say?

Manuel watched the snow gently falling outside the storefront windows. The lights around the edges of the windows twinkled on and off like tiny stars. In the peace and stillness of the moment, Manuel felt a jab of hope in his heart. There was something he had not considered: *what if the reversal had not been successful?* He had not gone back to the church to check on the results. Perhaps his most magnificent creation still drew breath.

While Manuel was trying to maintain his tentative hold on this shred of hope, the phone rang. At first, he didn't answer, wishing that the caller would give up. Manuel did not want to talk to anyone, he did not want his hope dashed by someone's urgent reality. Perhaps he could hold onto his hopeful feeling through the insistent ringing. But it was too late, the feeling was gone. Now he was glad the phone was ringing. He felt lonely and wanted to hear the sound of another human voice.

"Botanica," he said into the receiver.

Before anyone even spoke, he knew who it was. I will get no rest from this case until I am in my grave, he thought.

* * * * *

During his fall, Henry did not see his life flash before his eyes. An introspective man, he had already examined his life many, many times.

During his fall, Henry did not think of death or the imminent Judgement Day. He just took in the sights. The city beneath him, a giant twinkling jewel; the snow, a tapestry of lace. Henry felt as if he were inside his favorite childhood toy: the glass ball that you shook to see snow falling amid a peaceful scene of a church and a tiny village.

As a child, he'd always wanted to get inside this glass ball with its gently falling snow and its soothing scenery. He imagined himself as a tiny participant in the scene: making snowmen, sliding down hills on a sled, climbing the spire of the church all the way to the blue heaven painted on the top of the glass.

Henry's life had borne no resemblance to this tranquil childhood fantasy. He had lived on the edge, amid wars, social unrest, strife, and turmoil. But, in the midst of it all, he had kept a serene center, as if he had taken the glass ball into his heart's core.

Dum vivimus, vivamus, Henry thought. While we are living, let us live to the full.

During his fall, Henry felt complete—he needed nothing, he wanted nothing.

Henry was getting his first taste of eternity.

* * * * *

"Señora Vega," Manuel began. But, as usual, he could not get a word in. He held the phone away from his ear and listened to Emilia's mother weep, wail, and tell him that her poor child had disappeared.

"Disappeared? You mean, you saw her vanish?" Manuel said, feeling a jab of hope. Perhaps he would be delivered from the burden of this case, after all.

But it was not to be. Señora Vega, through sobs and gasping breaths, soon explained that the child was missing, gone from her bed, gone from the house. Emilia had gone searching, Señora Vega was sure, for dirt to eat.

"Yes, yes, Señora Vega," Manuel said. "Please call the police. They will find the child."

Of course, she told him, the police are already looking. But Señora Vega doubted that they would find her poor Emilia. Only the brujo could do that. "Por favor, brujo, por favor," Señora Vega sobbed.

It always came down to this. You spent ninety percent of your time on one case. Cases that did not pay. Cases that caused you to lose sleep and your hair to turn gray. Cases that drew black circles of weariness under your eyes. Cases that took away your appetite, and, when you did eat, gave you gas pains. Cases that caused you to cry out for mercy, that took the very joy out of living.

Manuel asked himself why he continued with this burdensome case, but he knew very well why. He thought very highly of himself; if he refused, he would not be able to hold himself in such high regard. The brujo was never more full of himself than when he was doing something against his will.

"I'll see what I can do," he said.

CHAPTER 23

The Big Kahuna

Not for a moment did Norma believe she was seeing things. She implicitly trusted her sanity, her practical turn of mind. She did not see things that weren't there. When things were there, they were really there. Hadn't her encounter with the Saints proven this?

There in the sky is a radiant being with a golden trumpet, she thought. I would be an idiot if I did not recognize this as the Judgement Day scenario—the actor, the setting, the prop, all there. But somewhere inside, Norma did not believe it. She felt as if she were witnessing a theatrical performance, and not an actual event.

Something was not quite right about the scene. And when Norma looked up, she knew what it was.

* * * * *

Tyler was the highest object in the sky. He hovered above the Sears Tower, where radio antennae projected into space. Tyler remembered the grating rock music that he'd been forced to listen to during his shift at the mini-mart. WSRM, or "The Scream," boasted frequently during its broadcasts that its antenna stood atop the world's tallest building. Not anymore, Tyler thought, as he reached down, plucked out the antenna, and hurled it to the ground. "Tower of babble," he bellowed as the antenna shot to earth.

Tyler had started out in life as puny, ugly, and powerless. Now he was big, beautiful, and powerful. He could inflict his revenge on everyone who had ever picked on him, refused him a job. He was now the biggest cheese of all. Combination football hero, CEO,

President of the United States, King of England, and John Wayne. He had the power to hire and fire.

Now Tyler was about to blow the horn of Judgement Day, and he would get the ultimate revenge on everyone. During his former life, weak and powerless, he had tried to be good. Now, in his omnipotent incarnation, he was about to brandish his terrible swift sword. If power corrupts, and God has the ultimate power, well, what then?

Had God gone insane with power? Had His mind split? What could mankind do to bring God back to His senses?

* * * * *

Ashes to ashes, thought Father Jeremiah Flynn as he surveyed the smoldering ruins of the church. He'd just returned from giving the Cardinal a full report.

"Was it arson?" asked His Eminence.

"No," Jeremiah replied.

"Are you sure?"

"No one in the neighborhood would burn the church."

"Someone from outside the neighborhood, then."

"And who would that be? God?"

The Cardinal dismissed this remark and moved on. "We were still insured. Perhaps this was a blessing in disguise."

The Cardinal's simplistic assessment made Jeremiah's blood boil and his face flush. These religious types, he thought. Always invoking *God's Will, For the Best, Blessings in Disguise, Blind Acceptance.*

When do we start to fight back? Rail at fate? Rail at God? When do we stand up and say: ENOUGH!

"This certainly solves your problem," Jeremiah finally said.

The Cardinal knew what Jeremiah meant. He had been absolved of making a controversial decision. He would not have to force Sacred Heart church to close. The fire had done that for him.

Now, as Jeremiah waded through the smoking rubble, he thought: I wonder what happened to my trump card?

* * * * *

"Do I have your attention?" Tyler boomed from the sky.

And where were our players?

Esperanza and Julio were holding hands outside the Round-the-Clock Donut Shoppe.

Danuta, Leszek, and Jarvis were holding hands on their front porch.

Norma was on the sidewalk, somewhere between the hospital and the charred shell of Sacred Heart.

Manuel was in Isabel Park, looking for Emilia.

Father Jeremiah Flynn was standing in the ruins.

The Cardinal was watching the Tonight Show.

But this was the ultimate Tonight Show: Judgement Day.

And where was Henry Purcell, the voice of heaven?

Where was the voice of reason in an unreasoning world?

Writing the final chapter of *Mixed Messages*.

CHAPTER 24

Keeping Time

Like a cat, Henry had landed on his feet. But the momentum of the fall had propelled him right into the bowels of the earth. When his velocity wound down, Henry found himself underground, on the platform of the Washington stop of the Howard/Jackson Park subway line.

He reeled, then sat on a blue bench carved with gang graffiti. He tried to collect his thoughts. All he could remember was his book. His darling book. Suddenly, he had an urgent sense that he had to finish it. Right away. Time was getting short.

Since Henry wasn't privy to the dramatic events happening in the sky outside, he had no idea how short time was in fact getting.

He reached into his pants pocket and found a small notebook and a short pencil. He absently noted his green workman's clothes, but the fact didn't register. Henry was oddly detached. He observed, but didn't judge. Didn't put two and two together. He saw, but didn't think.

He started to write. It was quiet, yet Henry didn't wonder at the lack of roaring trains, which Tyler had frozen in their tracks above ground. Still, trains became a starting point for Henry's final chapter.

Mixed Messages

The Final Chapter

Time is like a train. One event, one car after another. We experience this life as a narrative, a story. Things happen. There are beginnings, middles, endings. We frame this experience, this life, in time. It is only through the telling that we exist. We are a story in the mind of God.

"There shall be time no longer," it says in Revelations. *What does this mean? That we will finally experience the whole and not just the parts?*

The Bible speaks of the mind of God. So, then, can God lose His mind? Go mad? Go insane?

Is religion our way of placating an unstable deity?

What is religion? A story of God. What is worship? The theater of God. What is God? The ultimate playwright, the ultimate novelist. We are players in His story. Actors in His dreams.

Mixed messages: our heart speaks, our mind speaks. Which do we heed? How do we tell one voice from the other?

It is the end of the twentieth century. The churches are collapsing, religion is splintering. Still, people seek a spiritual life, seek spiritual food.

I have visited the crumbling temples. I have watched candles burn. I have heard the prayers of the faithful. I have smelled the incense. I have knelt on marble floors. I have prostrated myself before the Almighty. I have entered the holy of holies. I have spoken the name of God.

I have listened to the musical masters. Wept at the sheer beauty of a certain note. Felt the air for it, after it had faded.

Only in music can you achieve perfection. I know this. Don't ask me to tell you how or why.

Man longs for union. For a time, the great religions and the great music helped man unite with something greater. Perhaps this time is no longer.

Music is time. Time in all its glory. Time objectified. Time expressing itself in form.

The notes march across the page. We mark their time. We bring the flute to our lips, and the minutes and seconds come forth as music. You're early. You're late. You're on time. There is no in-between in music.

So while we still have time, Baby, let's jam.

CHAPTER 25

The Jam Session

It was the trumpet that had caught Norma's attention. It was the trumpet that was not quite right. Not the shiny, golden horn of judgement. But a dented and battered instrument, as if it had been passed down from musician to musician since the time the angels had first played.

Norma stopped walking, realizing where her feet had taken her. She was at "Saints and Saviors." When she walked inside, her sobbing flock ran to her.

"Sister Angelina! Save us!"

"Quick," Norma told them. "Get something to bang on and go outside."

* * * * *

Tyler raised the horn of Judgement Day and started to blow. The sound surprised him.

Not the doleful note he had expected. Not frightening or final or full of rueful judgement.

No, the sound was sweet.

And a strange thing happened to the people below. They weren't afraid. They weren't on their knees. They weren't repenting for their sins.

No, they were tapping their feet. And they had an urge. A powerful urge to play along.

They dug through closets, found dime-store guitars with strings missing. Got out the pots and pans and wooden spoons. Put toilet paper on combs. Blew the dust out of harmonicas. Found kazoos in toy boxes.

And they went outside—on porches, on sidewalks, in the middle of the street. In parks, on the frozen beach, in backyards, in school yards.

And they started to play.

And the sound was sweet.

* * * * *

Tyler hadn't counted on this. He had expected, well, a more solemn greeting. He had expected the dead to rise, the rivers to reverse their course. Instead, he got a jam session.

The music rose and filled his ears, the ears of God. And God wept. Wept at the perfection of it, the beauty. Music, the voice of heaven.

* * * * *

Henry placed a last period on the page and closed the notebook.

He heard music. Norma was nearby, he knew it. And he would find her. He knew it. He climbed the subway stairs, and the music hit him like a blast of warm air.

And such music! As if Time, all of Time, from beginning to end, were telling all, everything that had happened throughout the ages.

Now, children, Time was saying, let me tell you a story.

And the horns blew, the strings swelled, the pianos pounded. And the drums beat like the heart of God.

* * * * *

It was the drums. The very first instrument. The oldest, the best. Their steady boom, boom, boom rose and filled God's ears. He heard the sound of his own heart. Beating steadily.

And He returned to His senses.

Hallelujah.

* * * * *

Despite the musical extravaganza, Emilia was on a straight course to her goal. Obsessions, after all, brook no distractions.

* * * * *

Tyler's heart beat and beat, faster and faster. And with each beat, his heart grew larger, as if it were a tire being filled with air. He remembered a story he'd read about a child who'd been born with her heart outside her chest. He felt as if his heart, too, would burst through his body.

His heart lifted him higher and higher in the night sky. He saw a red glow above him, then he saw it: a thorny, Sacred Heart—huge and imposing in the sky. Now he was near it. Tyler reached out and took hold of the thorny branches. With two hands, he pulled with all his strength until the branches broke free and evaporated into the night.

Then the Sacred Heart opened like a huge heart locket. Inside, there was a family picture of Deeanna, Charlie, Eva, and the old Tyler. Then the picture changed to his brothers and sisters. Still another picture: person after person he had waited on at the minimart. He saw Leszek and Danuta and Jarvis standing on their porch. He saw the faces of the people from his neighborhood. He saw the faces of people he was sure he had never met. Face after face he saw in the Sacred Heart. Then the heart got smaller and smaller, until it was the size of a locket. Tyler took hold of the locket, held it to his chest, and began his slow descent to the ground.

* * * * *

Emilia walked past the weeping priest playing the violin and climbed the stone steps. Inside, the roof was gone. But below, on the ground, yes! It was there.

She reached down her tiny hand and scooped up the ashes. Then she raised her hand to her lips.

The taste was sweet.

Acknowledgments

Hello, night owls, this is Henry Purcell. I have as my guest the author of *Tales of the Sacred Heart*.

Hello, Henry.

Tell us about the book, Mel.

First, I'd like to thank a few people.

Go right ahead.

Homero Adame and Jorge Adame kindly shared their magical ways with me—though I took a great deal of artistic license with the information.

So, they told you about all the potions and stuff?

Right. Jennifer Hennen introduced us. She was also gracious enough to take me on a tour of Chicago churches and Milwaukee Avenue botanicas.

That girl gets around.

So does her mother, Laura Meng, an actress who brought to life a play I wrote.

Tell us about it.

The play was called Cowboy Pictures, *and it was about my Grandmother. She was the one who made me want to become a writer.*

Write any other plays?

Quite a few. I was a founding member of the Chicago Dramatists Workshop. It was Karolus Smejda's idea to create the workshop. When he asked me to work with him, it started me on a new path.

Ever write any other books?

A children's book called The Cabbage Man. *Colleen Delegan read it and gave me my first break as a creative writer. I owe her a lot.*

What got you thinking about the millennium?

When I was about ten, my Uncle, John DuBouchet, told me I'd live to see the turn of the century. I tried to imagine what it would be like.

Anybody else who inspired you?

My aunt, Esther Schneiter. Everything she did was a work of art.

Where'd you learn about fires?

I talked to Myron Kovalevych, a Chicago firefighter. Though, if I've made any mistakes, they're all mine. I'd also like to thank his wife, Carol, for her warm hospitality.

How did you meet them?

Through one of my oldest friends, Sharon Farrell, a wonderful artist, whose joie de vivre has been a source of inspiration.

That preacher woman, Sister Merlina Talbott, was wild. How did you come to make her up?

My oldest friend, Kathleen Dunleavy, took me to a revival meeting.

How did you dream up the part about Norma and the public transportation ads?

I got the idea from my mother, Margaret Werner. She used to try to find an ad that contained the entire alphabet as she rode the subway. My mother searched for the alphabet because she loved to read—and she shared her love of books with me.

What about Jarvis, the judge?

Nathan Miller told me some stories about a judge—but, of course, it's entirely coincidental if Jarvis bears any resemblance to any person living or dead.

Who am I based on?

While some people may feel you were based on a famous Chicago radio personality, I must say that it is entirely coincidental if you, or any of the characters in the book, bear any resemblance to any person living or dead. Though my stepfather, Hub Werner, shares your youthful spirit—and is blessed with an endless supply of jokes.

You seem to really love music.

It's my first love. I'd like to thank the musicians in my life: Steve Vazquez, my guitar teacher; and Steve Hashimoto, my partner and soulmate—a truly great jazz musician, who opened my ears and my heart.

Since music is so important to you, it seems fitting that your novel was released by Bogfire, a company that also publishes recordings of Blues and Celtic music.

Jim Fraher and Connie Scanlon, the founders of Bogfire, are doing a great job of keeping the Blues and other rare music alive. I owe them a great debt of thanks for their faith in this book. Special thanks to Connie for her beautiful design, and her enormous heart and depth of soul.

How did you come up with Leszek and Danuta?

Over the years, I've lived in several buildings with Polish landlords. I love Polish people—all the ones I've known have been very emotional, soulful, funny, and interesting.

Where'd you grow up, Mel?

In Humboldt Park and Bucktown—two inner-city Chicago neighborhoods. I'd like to thank my neighbors from the old days for sharing their stories.

Anybody else you'd like to thank?

My children, Jessica Villines and Joel Villines. They're the light of my life. I love them with all my heart.

Mel, how did you get started writing this book?

I was washing my hands one day and, in the mirror before me, I saw a giant mural with a church, a radio station, and all the characters in the book. A line came into my head, and I wrote it down. Then more lines came, and I wrote them down. After a while, I had a book.

What type of soap were you using?

The liquid kind from a dispenser. I don't know the brand.

How did it smell?

The smell was sweet.

That's sort of how the novel ends.

Yes.

The taste was sweet.

Very.
